About the Author

David Bohr is an engineer, and writer, who is passionate about astrophysics and art. In this he decided to portray a fantastic and epic story to delight people who love reading. David Bohr likes the natural passages, hiking, and practicing sports. He believes life is like a short novel, which must be lived as a long tale. David Bohr lives with his beloved wife.

Starlight and the Magic Universes

David Bohr

Starlight and the Magic Universes

Vanguard Press

VANGUARD PAPERBACK

© Copyright 2024
David Bohr

The right of David Bohr to be identified as author of
this work has been asserted by him in accordance with the
Copyright, Designs and Patents Act 1988.

All Rights Reserved

No reproduction, copy or transmission of this publication
may be made without written permission.
No paragraph of this publication may be reproduced,
copied or transmitted save with the written permission of the
publisher, or in accordance with the provisions
of the Copyright Act 1956 (as amended).

Any person who commits any unauthorised act in relation to
this publication may be liable to criminal
prosecution and civil claims for damages.

A CIP catalogue record for this title is
available from the British Library.

ISBN 978 1 83794 022 6

This is a work of fiction. Names, characters, businesses, places, events and
incidents are either the product of the author's imagination or used in a
fictitious manner. Any resemblance to actual persons, living or dead, or actual
events is purely coincidental.

Vanguard Press is an imprint of
Pegasus Elliot Mackenzie Publishers Ltd.
www.pegasuspublishers.com

First Published in 2024

Vanguard Press
Sheraton House Castle Park
Cambridge England

Printed & Bound in Great Britain

Be the Light

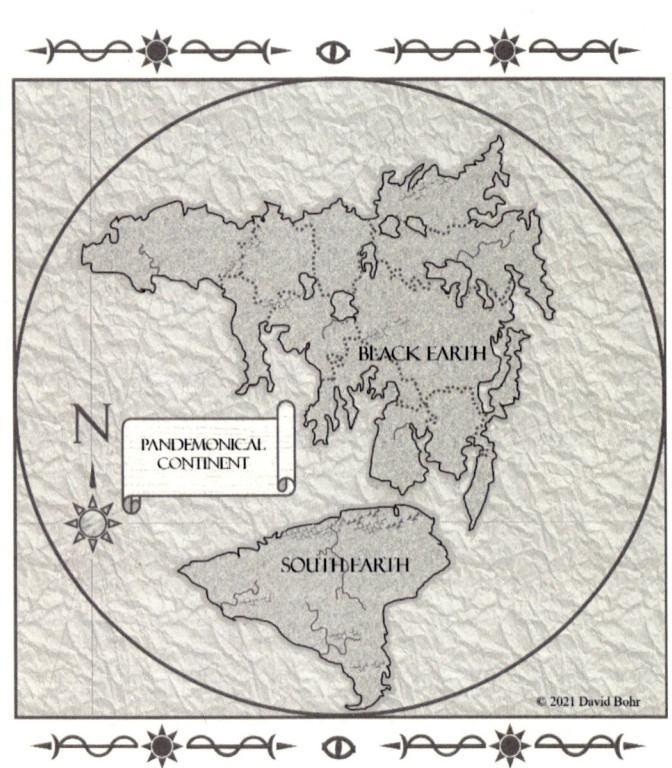

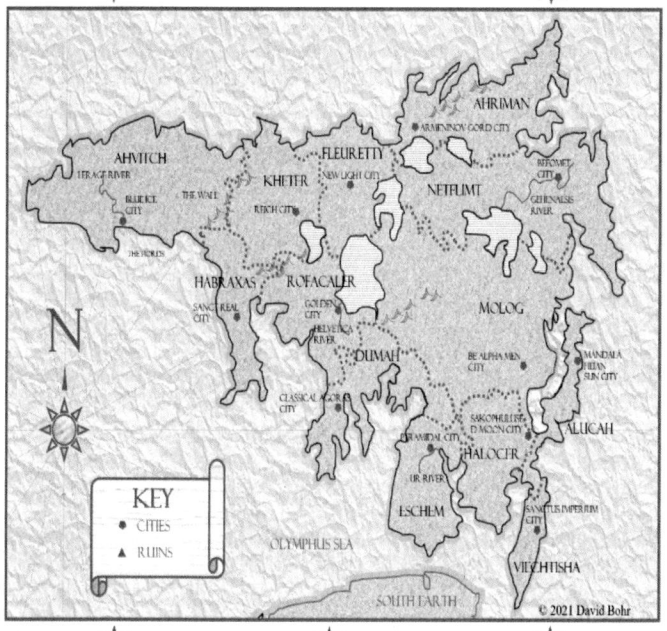

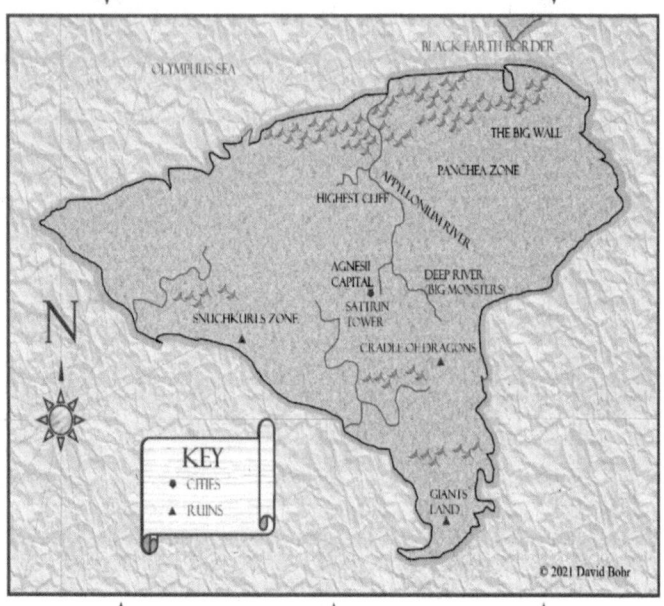

PROLOGUE

A noisy beep was disturbing the peace inside the dark capsule. There were many lights emitting from some of the buttons on the pod's master control board. Those lights denoted an unusual language compounded by symbols of stars and suns of turquoise colour. The frontal window of that spaceship showed many orange clouds as a cumulus of fire passing swiftly.

In another place, there were two beings of grey skin with insectoid appearance looking through an enormous window in a dark room. They were enjoying the view of a city whose lights seemed like fire laces. Its metal buildings were inclined as if they were embedded.

"Has the capsule arrived at the farm yet?" one of the two beings asked the other one.

"It was impacted, but it is still maintaining its course. We are tracking the possible landing area."

"Have they done that attack?"

"No, they have not. It was executed by one of our allies who dwells in that place. The self-called Farmer."

"Those replicas are extremely competitive between them, even to attack a baby. However, it does not matter. In any event, we will win."

CHAPTER ONE

The Water Curtain Silhouette

On a winter night decorated with brilliant stars, a poor couple in a big city discovered a baby in a basket. The serpent star was in the firmament that night. It was a lovely gift provided by the Ophiuchus Constellation. That basket had a dark turquoise mantle of the Nebra civilization. The cloth was embroidered with golden figures of many stars, a sun and the baby's name as well. The mantle covered that precious infant, who was warm within it. His name was Starlight, and the couple accepted him as their son. They gave him all their love.

Many moons passed since that night and Starlight's childhood was happily cared for by his adoptive family. He had grown up, and his adolescence had arrived. He obtained a scholarship to study at the most prestigious private high school in the world. That institution was Beliar High School located in Befomet City. One of those days in class, Starlight was formulating some equations of the universe expansion on the blackboard. They represented bizarre symbols for most people, but not for him. It was not strange for his professor to see Starlight's skills when developing those formal proofs.

Starlight was a little freak and a bad boy at the same time. He was the centre of attention because of his high scores. Girls talked to him because he was so handsome and had an exceptional mind as well.

That afternoon, Starlight left his classes and took his bicycle riding it under an intense storm. Suddenly, he stopped and gazed at a thin water curtain, which fell from a bridge. An inconspicuous silhouette was there. It was like a ghost, which was seeing him. Starlight whispered and left behind his bike. Then, he walked towards that little fall. He touched the water curtain with his index finger. At the other side of that water stele, the silhouette was trying to touch the fall as well. At last, their fingers touched each other. The storm rose, and a vast explosion occurred. It was like a sinusoidal wave and thousands of raindrops leapt through the air. After that collapse, everything was confusing, and Starlight appeared laid on a bed in the Befomet City Hospital. That medical centre had visible white bricks and small violet hanging flowers at its exterior walls.

Starlight opened his eyes and noticed he was in the hospital.

I was nearing the bridge. How did I come here? he thought.

The silhouette appeared next to a transparent window, outside of that hospital room. Then, the mysterious figure in the window vanished. Suddenly, a nurse entered that chamber. She had a lovely pale face and black hair. She was dressed in a white gown with a purple shield embroidered on her chest at the left side. That shield had the shape of a snake at its centre. It was the Befomet City Hospital insignia.

"How do you feel Mr Starlight?" the nurse asked.

"Fine my young lady." Starlight was still stunned about how he got incorporated on the bed. "What happened to me?"

Starlight was worried trying to remember the last event paying no attention to that youthful and sensual nurse. She was looking at him with her precious grey eyes and thinking about how handsome he was.

"Mr Starlight you see, hear and be silent. You had a fainting from a low sugar level. However, you can leave in a few minutes. Your pressure and sugar level are in optimal conditions."

"Thank you."

Since Starlight was a child he suffered from fainting episodes. In most cases those events occurred before he fell asleep. Starlight began hearing a loud noise (as great as a boat). Then, he felt waves entering his body. Finally, that boy always woke up with his throat so dry. His adoptive family did not know about it. In fact, nobody knew it. That was his secret.

Days and nights borne and vanished, and time passed like a standard rule of the existence. During that period, Starlight was worried about his few possibilities to pay for a university program. Related to that, a miracle happened on a rainy afternoon a few days before his high school graduation. Royal Imperium University dispatched an officer to talk to the Beliar High School principal. That university would offer a scholarship to Starlight.

Royal Imperium University was in Befomet City as well. As its name suggested, that institution was for the elite. Every son coming from the aristocracy and royal families must study there.

The education and illumination were important themes for Starlight. In fact, there was a proverb of a prominent philosopher from the Kether Region, and it was Starlight's slogan. That quote was the following:

The beings are just that the education could do for them, and no more. Otherwise, they could not follow the light's paths.

The university officer was with the Beliar High School's board and Starlight was giving a speech about scholar economics. He was in front of all the high school student's parents. After his speech, those adults applauded him with glee. At that point, a professor approached and informed him about the good news, the offering of the university grant.

Then, Starlight walked across a chiaroscuro corridor of that high school. It was adorned with purple and lilac flowers. At the end of that passage, he opened a first-century dark door. He was entering the principal's office.

Starlight felt an odd sensation. "*Grata ad solis ortum.*" He started listening to a chorus singing that verse together with screams of war. That phrase meant in ancient Leviathan language: welcome creator.

Then, a black ocean appeared in his mind. He gazed at the white velvet beach under a black sky. In that vision, there was a sun as timid as a full moon. Then, Starlight left that delusion and focused on the other side of the door.

In that room, there was neither the principal nor any member of the high school board. Instead, there was a young man waiting for him.

"Good morning, Mr Starlight. I am T. Aroth, officer of Royal Imperium University. I came today representing the most prestigious college…"

Again, in Starlight's mind were those unusual scenes and voices. However, he was paying attention to Mr Aroth.

"…Mr Starlight, are you ready to initiate your studies at Sanctum Real Advanced Mathematics School?"

At that moment, Starlight took out a note from his bag and gave it to Mr Aroth. That note was a speech written by him about a mathematical model to improve the wealth of poor people. Mr Aroth read it amazed. Then, that officer focused his gaze at Starlight.

"My Lord, you should enter the Mological Economics School rather than the Sanctum Real School of Mathematics. This note will be so interesting for your student application and the Congress."

"The Congress?" Starlight asked.

"Patience, my Lord. Everything in due course."

"If you said so, it would be fine. I have a question. Should I sign some issues?"

"You must wait for instructions my Lord."

"Thank you, Mr Aroth."

Another day had come, and a blue-sky showed so clear its face. A mighty noise from a combat plane broke that tranquillity. Many fighters, tanks and the infantry were in the thirteen capital cities of Black Earth. The sky had a gala with the Death Angels (combat planes). One of those fighters crossed the sky in a diagonal way. It produced at its mark a steam stele. Starlight was amazed seeing that parade, admiring those tanks and fighters. That day was the date of Black Earth's freedom celebration.

The Leviathan family (the first imperial lineage) were placed in Black Earth's territories and established both Royal Imperium University and Beliar High School at the beginning of time. The first member of that family, (a man of thirty-three years of age) went with a little army towards South Earth. He created an allegiance with the deities of that part of the world. So, that Leviathan rebel betrayed his ancestors and became the leader of South Earth creatures, the Agnesii. Since that moment, that race declared a war against the peaceful land of the imperial family.

After that episode in Black Earth's history, those Leviathans became Hur-Appeans. They evolved in their social structure and technology. In that way they were ready to end the war. The Lord of Lords, General Be Alpha Men liberated Black Earth on the twenty-second day of the sixth month of the thirty-third year. That general fought with his Hur-Appean soldiers against the South Earth army and won that war, killing the Leviathan traitor. So, each year in all territories of Black Earth, people commemorated that date with splendorous parades. The army and police participated in those events exhibiting their best armaments.

One month after that parade, Starlight was at his house in his modest room when his adoptive father entered. He gave a letter to his son. The sunlight entered through Starlight's room window caressing the teenager's black hair. Starlight clutched the letter from his father's hand. Then, father and son hugged each other. Starlight started reading that message:

Royal Imperium University and the Mological School of Economics are delighted to inform you have been accepted as a new student. Furthermore, you have been awarded with the scholarship: Excelsiur Lux et Geo...

Two months later, Starlight started studying at Royal Imperium University. That institution had big castles on its campus, ancient architecture, and walls with hanging flowers. Early in the morning, the fog in the yard passed rounding its buildings (castles) and its big cypresses. All constructions of that university had their columns and porches decorated with golden coloured figures of intertwined snakes, horse heads and fleurs-de-lys. At the northwest cardinal point, that university had an enormous croissant shaped lake. At the centre of its campus, there were more castles allocated in a unique design. Those constructions were in a vast circular area creating the shape of an owl with its wings opened (from an aerial view). Many trees and five vehicular ways rounded the prime circular area, which denoted a pentagon.

On Starlight's first day of classes, there were many students walking on the campus. On his way, Starlight discovered a statue of General Be Alpha Men. That sculpture was seated and its right hand showed the sky as a signal of victory. The middle and ring fingers of that hand were pointing downwards and the rest upwards. Its other hand exhibited the ground to remain the oldest light enemies: the Agnesii. Below the statue's feet there was an inscription:

Hic est domus be alpha men.

Behind that statue was the Mological School of Economics. In front of it, there was a massive bull statue made of gold between two marble columns with an inscription at its base:

Omnia est unum.

Starlight continued walking towards his classroom with other students. Suddenly, he gazed at his watch. Its dial incorporated a symbol of a triquetra as decoration. Starlight opened his eyes amazed and started running to enter the school of economics building. There, he ran in a clockwise way up the rectangular stairs of black and white colour. Then, he arrived at his schoolroom for the class of Theoretical Economy at Imperial Invasion. There, Starlight saw the blackboard filled with differential equations for dynamic macroeconomic analysis. He sat down on his chair but got up even faster. Starlight took the chalk and started developing the proofs of those theorems. He did it until the end, clean and perfect. To him it felt like writing a poem.

Again, the strange bridge figure appeared, imperceptible at a window of that classroom. For a while, it looked at Starlight. Then, it vanished rapidly.

The time was passing, and Starlight won friends, recognition, and a joyful life in the university.

Six semesters later, he was in his college room reading a book called, *Trívium et Quadrivium*.

At that moment, his room phone started ringing. "Hello... is there an invitation for me to visit Senator Malmo? Must I receive it in the university principal's office? Well, I am going to go there. Thank you."

Starlight left his building and then crossed a path made of stone. That paved corridor was near an ancient church, which was a library. There, Starlight felt some waves entering his body. He did not pay attention to them because that event was familiar to him. He continued walking towards the school's main office. Once Starlight arrived, he spoke for a few minutes with the principal of the university. Then, he left that building. Starlight went so happy, thinking about his meeting with Senator Malmo.

Two days later, a diplomatic limousine and some motorcycle guards arrived at Royal Imperium University. That caravan would transport Starlight towards Black Earth's Congress which was called Lexabyssi. That government area had constructions with vast gardens. The main edifice had ochre walls and three domes on its roof. There were three military attack helicopters, many security teams, and soldiers around that sector. In that building, some congressional representatives were talking about macroeconomics, decisions, and public policies. They were on a long corridor full of justice sculptures.

After his limousine trip and the congress entrance protocol, Starlight arrived at that corridor. There, the youthful student opened an office door and saw Senator Malmo. He was sitting on his chair with his legs crossed. The chair was made of gold with many trimmings. The senator's feet did not touch the floor as if he did not want to be on that nasty earth. Starlight gazed at him and recalled a photograph taken by a famous artist from the Ahriman Region, whose name was Notemkhim.

"Good morning, Senator Malmo," Starlight said.

"Morning," Malmo answered, looking at him in a polite way. That senator continued, "Morning is a word, but some words are not certain. Life is the truth, as science, and mind."

"Mind is grandeur, mind is all, and mind is beautiful. A word is a part of a language, but only the language per se is nothing. It needs a channel, emissary, receptor and at least a message. Language is nothing without understanding or knowledge. Science is knowledge, and knowledge is the universe's essence. It is the same concept as reality Senator Malmo," Starlight replied.

"So clever Mr Starlight. Albeit we are not hither to philosophise, we are here to face political life situations. People require rules, order, and guidance. It is the natural path of life Mr Starlight."

"Senator Malmo, we are here for them. We are here to give them a small treasure called justice."

"Policy is not merely like economics Mr Starlight…"

"Senator Malmo…" Starlight interrupted him. "Policy is a part of knowledge, which intrinsically involves mathematics, economics, laws, and philosophy."

Mr Malmo looked at him so annoyed. He took Starlight's curriculum vitae and read it so disdainfully. "You are so smart Mr Starlight. You are the first of your college to obtain the highest qualifications," Malmo continued seeing him in an inquisitive way. "How do you comprehend all Mr Starlight?"

"I do not know, sir. Science and arts taught me how to handle them, on my mind."

"Mr Starlight, you do not know how many times I asked that question. You do not know how many times I listened to that answer."

"The most substantial thing is to know how many times you identified that response was true."

Malmo was extremely pleased with that answer. "This Earth requires a leader like you, Mr Starlight. These days are threatening days. Do you see yourself as a part of my staff?"

"Of course, it will be a great honour."

"No boy, the honour is mine. I will communicate with your counsellor Mr Aroth to coordinate your role in my team. Thank you for your time, Mr Starlight. You already know the exit way. Have a nice day."

A deep friendship borne between that senator and Starlight from that meeting. Through time, Starlight became Malmo's right hand man. Which made the young apprentice enormously popular in the congress and media.

The senator was a lone man because his family had died in mysterious circumstances. Therefore, the experienced politician saw Starlight like a member of his family. Malmo used to say to him, "I am going to tell you my father's favourite phrase. Do what thou wilt but do it with the light. Through the darkest hour, you must learn how to be the light and the guide of the universe."

Each day, Starlight continued studying his career in economics. In parallel, he produced scientific advances in most areas as well. He donated all his research to Royal Imperium University and Beliar High School. On one of those days, Starlight left the university library. He went towards his college room to take a rest. Suddenly, a dark luxury sports car arrived there. A strange figure was spying on Starlight from that auto. A few minutes later, the gorgeous car went away.

At that moment, Starlight did not notice the spy car because many people were greeting him, whilst he was walking on the campus.

Then, he arrived at his room and many images started glimpsing in his mind. They were related about how to create a multidimensional, space-time mass transmitter using a powerful tool provided by science. Everything in the universe can be represented as vectors. They can travel through a perpendicular axis, forming twists upwards and downwards. If that axis is the time and those vectors could be people, they can travel across the time. However, he would need something more than theory to convert those principles into a tangible thing.

After that consideration, he laid down on his bed because he was so tired. Suddenly, Starlight felt some waves entering his body. A train sound started filling his ears. He felt that his throat was so dry, and his soul could move in circles in his body.

"I am in a dream. It is untrue," Starlight babbled.

He gazed at both sides and found some shapes as fogs of black and orange colour. At that point, Starlight listened to guttural voices. He looked at his hands and feet, and they started to move like elastic gums. Then, he jumped so fast and high. While Starlight was flying, he approached a nearby window. Suddenly, he crashed into it producing a rain of crystal pieces, which fell from the top of the towering skyscraper of the Daedric Bank building.

Instead of Starlight going out from that smashed window, a black superbike at high-speed performing a jump did. That competition bike was driven by a pilot dressed in black leather clothes. Those broken glasses continued falling and the superbike produced a smoke tale from its rear wheel. The racing bike and its pilot landed on the roof of a building in front of Daedric Bank.

Meanwhile, a black attack helicopter was approaching near that area and the sun of a new day appeared in the sky. From that chopper, someone released a length cord over the superbike pilot. That bike driver performed a tremendous, supernatural, and acrobatic jump to catch it. The superbike fell from the building crashing against the pavement creating a sinusoidal wave explosion.

The superbike pilot caught that cord hanging from the chopper, landing on another skyscraper's roof. The superbike pilot's black helmet reflected a silhouette of a crow flying.

Suddenly, a Black Earth Science Agency (BESA) fighter appeared. The combat plane pilot was communicating with his headquarters.

"There is a non-registered attack helicopter flying low, near the city centre."

"Commander White Owl places the alien chopper on your target. Give it the order to abandon the urban area, make it twice. In case of a second negative or not answering, proceed to open fire."

"Roger that."

A few moments later, the invader attack helicopter did not respond to the second warning. The BESA fighter launched a torpedo against that intruder chopper causing an explosion in the sky. The superbike pilot's head turned at the other side of the blast to see a diplomatic caravan, which was approaching. The explosion continued moving the sky like water waves.

The superbike pilot jumped from the skyscraper roof and fell into a standing position on a car in movement, curving it like a piece of bubble gum. Then, that pilot jumped towards other cars until fell on the limousine of the diplomatic caravan. That government car had two Black Earth flags on its frontal part. They had a white background and a cross of cyan colour. At the centre of the flag, there was a golden double-head eagle embroidered. The bird held in its claws an inscription:

Deus nobiscum.

The superbike pilot broke the windshield of that car, and then vanished as stardust and passed through the frontal smashed window. Once on the limousine, the superbike pilot continued using the helmet. That pilot took out two automatic guns and pointed them at ninety degrees of separation. One pistol had the trajectory to the limousine driver and the other one to Senator Malmo (who was sitting in the back seat). The window that divided the driver and limousine guest part was downwards. Hence, the superbike pilot put both the senator and his driver on target.

"This is my space, you Hur-Appean," the superbike pilot said with a robotic voice.

"This is my time, you Asdomii," Senator Malmo answered.

Simultaneously, a golden bullet left each one of those ᵐᵘns, leaving a wave stele behind them. One bullet reached Senator Malmo's forehead, crossing his head, and then breaking the rear window of the limousine.

"This is my body," the superbike pilot said.

The other bullet reached the limousine driver's head. Then, the murderer who was in a squatting position opened the left frontal limousine door with a kick. It left so fast from that diplomatic car as if a dozen bulls stamped that door.

Behind the limousine was approaching a black luxury sports car (the same type as the spy auto at university campus). That modern car was dodging many bullets from Senator Malmo's guards. The sports car driver opened the left door. At the same time, the long diplomatic limousine went at excessive speed without control because its driver was dead. The superbike pilot jumped from the limousine towards the sports car. Once on that auto, that mysterious being launched a transparent barrier and closed the car door. That vehicle continued rolling on the lane. Then, the limousine of the senator crashed into the gel obstacle launched by the terrorist. The long black car exploded on the highway. Senator Malmo's guard limousines had the same ending.

Police patrols of Befomet City still pursued the black sports car. The BESA fighter performed a turn in the air ready to target the murderer's vehicle. That black sports car crossed another kind of transparent elastic field, then that automobile disappeared. Some patrols, which were pursuing the murderer, crashed into that transparent wall exploding as well. After that situation, the rare shield vanished.

Starlight woke up after his fainting episode. The clock in his room marked six-sixteen in the morning. That clock was made of wood. It had a black background and white clockwise rods. It exhibited a non-digital display with one inscription:

Khronos zeit.

Starlight got up from his bed and started walking when his room telephone rang. That device displayed a number on its screen: 1-44-000.

"Hello?"

"Good morning." Mr Aroth was on the other end. "My Lord, is necessary for your presence here in the Eshudical Room at the Congress, as soon as possible."

"I am going to go there right now."

Starlight hung up the phone. Then, he put on his new luxury dark imperial jacket and left his college residence. Outside of that students' building, there was a diplomatic car. Starlight had it at his service since he started to work in the congress.

It started to rain, and Starlight felt the raindrops falling on his head and face. The water drops touched his white face, his blue-sky eyes, and his plentiful black hair.

Starlight whispered and then he entered the black and long car. He asked the driver for a way toward the congress. A few seconds later, the limousine crossed near the big golden bull statue at Mological School. Behind it, the odd silhouette was seeing that diplomatic car fixedly.

Starlight's limousine wheels were rolling on the wet pavement cutting the water on the street. Meanwhile, that student remained the phrase: *Omnia est unum*. People in the university were running on the Nergal Bridge holding big umbrellas to avoid getting wet. The bridge had ochre bricks at its upper part and red bricks at its lower part. That construction received the impacts from the Gehenaesis River's flow. Starlight gazed at those long streets near the bridge through the limousine window.

Once Starlight arrived at the congress, he saw many black diplomatic vehicles. There, people were dressed in dark clothes and carried enormous brollies as well. Starlight descended from the limousine and looked at that entire panorama. He already foresaw something inevitable.

Mr Aroth received him. "My Lord; it's time. Come with me towards the Eshudical Room, it is necessary that you know something."

In that room, Starlight and Mr Aroth sat down on a luxurious big leather sofa.

"My Lord, Senator Malmo died a few hours ago." Mr Aroth took a breath and continued, "He was assassinated by terrorists from South Earth."

"That is impossible. He would be proclaimed as congress president."

"He was against South Earth's interests," Aroth said.

"Why? Why, so violence?"

"Well, in Malmo's will my Lord, he left an under oath note that his representation and political legacy must be yielded to you. Do you want to accept it?"

"Accept it? Are you insane Mr Aroth? I am not going to steal my master's political career. I am not an assassin. My passion is people, not death."

"Really, do you believe it Mr Starlight?"

"I just want to have a balance between life and science, expressed in mathematics and nature. On the other hand, I think…" Starlight stopped talking, then he whispered and gazed down. "All this would be in vain without someone with a resolute will, and capable to guide the society. Maybe, you have the reason Mr Aroth. I do not want to be the apprentice that takes advantage of his dead master. I just want to preserve his legacy…where is Senator Malmo, Mr Aroth?"

"My Lord, his body is in the Beltane-Imbolg Church here in Lexabyssi."

Rain continued falling and Starlight walked through a place with splendorous gardens, where there was a chapel with a ponderous frontal door. That church had rectangular windows decorated with branches, flowers, and swan shapes. Their wooden frames ended in arc shapes at their topmost part. Some flowers hung from them.

In another part of the city, a black crow flew over a street of Befomet City. Below its wings appeared thousands of black pieces of broken glasses giving turns as twists. All those pieces re-joined creating a luxury black sports car on that street. It was the same auto, which fled from Malmo's crime scene. Near it, in the same way appeared the superbike pilot, dressed in black leather clothes again. At that moment, the pilot had a white superbike. The big motorcycle and the sports car started rolling on so fast. They took a highway dodging the traffic. They arrived at the third level of a bridge. The sports car butted a tridem lorry, which broke the safety barrier. The white superbike rolled on the long container of that heavy vehicle, whilst it fell. The lorry, superbike and its pilot got to the second level bridge of the highway in a secure way. That big vehicle stopped its path and the superbike pilot continued going to the city centre. The luxury black sports car went on the third bridge level, pursued by police patrols.

Simultaneously, Starlight walked towards Beltane-Imbolg. Once more, the rain made a water stele, which fell from a narrow balcony at the top of a white tower of that church. Starlight approached near that water curtain so slowly, as if the entire universe seems to be stopping. Then, the world started moving in a reverse way. Rain rose from soil towards the heavens and then the water drops were suspended in the air. Starlight ascended from the three steps that were in front of that water stele. He pointed his index finger on that curtain. From the other side of that liquid wall appeared a tiny white index finger. It had a golden ring with an embedded turquoise gem, which had a butterfly shape. Those two fingers touched. Then, an explosion occurred. The birds were static on their fly, whilst the raindrops were thrown out by the blast.

Starlight appeared in a sunflower field under a cyan sky across the water stele. On that magnificent landscape, two beings were touching their index fingers against each other's. Starlight was one of those personages. He still wore his black imperial jacket decorated with golden edges, black satin trousers and golden boots. In front of him was the silhouette. Now it was so clear, that shadow was a person. She was a beautiful young girl with blonde hair like the sunshine. She had a white face and green eyes. That girl had a perfect well-shapely body covered by a semitransparent dress embroidered with purple and violet-blue flowers. She looked like a Sandrineum painting (Sandrine was a distinguished painter from the Habraxas Region). He pictured a lovely girl in a shell on the sea. Like in that painting, the fair-haired juvenile girl had a long lilac fabric girdle, which held on her two forearms and rounded her waist. In addition, she had golden queen shoes, tied for small-crossed straps. Those shoes contained diamonds and were embedded with rubies.

The water curtain silhouette. Starlight thought.

"Who are you?" he interrogated her.

"Silence my Lord. The men corrupted this planet, destruction, death and pollution are killing this world.

Each time when a planet is going to die it releases its last resource: the Nymphs."

"Pollution? I know a lot about natural conservation theory. Your argument is invalid. If the planet wants to exterminate us, it will activate all its volcanoes at the same time…" Starlight said.

"However," she interrupted him. "You represent the balance of the universe my young black hair Lord. Just allow me to hold your hand."

They took their hands and started dancing, whilst the wind rumbled sounds from a symphonic orchestra. The young couple danced on air given circles and started floating so slowly. Their bodies moved like stripes of paper giving turns. Those two beings became a white lotus flower, whilst they were dancing. The interior stem of that flower seemed like a black-green tube. Then, it transformed into a fractal channel of neon colours. That biological journey ended in the right eye of Malmo's apprentice.

By protocol, the guards could not be near Starlight when he was visiting Senator Malmo's body. For that reason, neither security-corps nor Mr Aroth realised the rendezvous between the boy and the Nymph (the water curtain blonde girl).

Starlight came from the meeting with the precious teenager outside of Beltane-Imbolg. Then, he entered the church where Senator Malmo's body was. Starlight's face was a little whiter. He was daunting due to the sadness of seeing his master. At that moment, Starlight nestled on the floor with his right hand on the coffin, which was at the church's central nave. The floor of the chapel was made of beige marble. It was decorated by one big figure of a lotus flower compounded by many black and white chiropterans. Then, Starlight stood up and left that chapel. At that instant, Mr Aroth arrived there.

"My Lord, art thou alright?"

"Yes, Mr Aroth. I vanished into my thoughts completely. A few minutes ago, I met with someone when I was…"

"My Lord, it is time for thy speech," Mr Aroth interrupted him.

"Thou hast the reason Mr Aroth."

Then, Starlight and his guards got into the limousine, which was in front of the chapel. They went from Beltane-Imbolg towards Tartarusm Square (the main square of the Congress). Meanwhile, Starlight was looking through the car window. He was thinking about being the youngest congress president in Black Earth's history. That fact would depend on the plenary elections.

Tartarusm Square was in front of the Pandemonical Building. That square had a rectangular white-water fountain at its centre. Many white and lilac magnolias were rounding its edges. The place was jammed with people, senators, diplomatic corps, journalists and students from Beliar High School and Royal Imperium University. One atrium of marble supported by two columns was placed at that square. Those columns ended in Venician chapiters

(Venici was a city of the Habraxas Region). On their base, there was a plate with the following inscription:

Beati luce.

Starlight left the limousine surrounded by his security guards and walked towards that atrium. He overheard unusual voices as a chorus, which was crooning. "*Grata ad solis ortum.*"

Just Starlight could hear them. His security members did not listen to that chorus. Starlight turned his head, but he could not see any of those mysterious singers. Therefore, he continued walking with his guards.

A young blond man of good height, white face, green eyes was preparing the microphone for Starlight. That man wore a black dress, a skinny black tie and white shirt. He was two years more than Starlight's age. That man was Mr Aroth.

The rain passed and the blue-sky covered Befomet City again. In heaven, there were some attack helicopters of black colour with armed soldiers on them. They were watching the crowd to assure their security. At that moment, a whisper broke the silence. Starlight took the microphone.

"My people, the unity of our race and our decisions are the unique way to make our dreams a reality. It is time to confront all our enemies. I came not here saying: I am going to change the world. I came here facing this moment with each one of you. Do not have any doubt to face any fear! It is a simple life decision: or we are together to get the commonwealth, or we left on other hands our present and future. Maybe the universe gives us one opportunity to lead our destiny, and it always does it through the darkest hour. Today, our people were offended, but we are not going to accept this kind of intimidation. Instead of that, we must preserve our freedom and unity as a society. Perhaps, people from South Earth despise us because every day we try to eradicate the greatest world sins: poorness, ignorance, violence, and segregation. We do it because it is the best way to develop a nation. Today, our women and men have this land and tomorrow will have our children. We will continue being a part of this earth forever, together with the power of our revolutionary youth. Today I come saying to each one of you: do what thou wilt but do it with the light. The wisdom goes forth in front of us, to erase all fears and adversities. We will get peace and will do it with the help of the gods. Thank you."

A roar of applause filled that place. Girls and dudes from colleges and high schools applauded Starlight. Meanwhile, older people were talking about his great charisma and eloquence. Some doves were flying in the sky, and the sun shone on the entire city. Starlight gazed at the blue firmament. He gave the order to the symphonic orchestra to start the requiem.

"We listen to the special honours for our master Malmo," Starlight said.

Under that clean sky, they were moving some dynamic buildings of a Befomet City borough called city centre. There a group of five buildings made of steel had at their basal part a platform with a small lake in that district. It had pedestrian ways with gorgeous trees as well. There was another dynamic building with the shape of a cylindrical tube, like a catenary against the soil. That building had silver and gold colours and its movements remained a worm leaving from soil. Aside from that, there was another construction, which moved in a sinusoidal way. Its shape was like the tail of a whale. Nearby, the rest of that artificial grampus was moving as if it was swimming into a green sea made of grass. The white superbike crossed that skyscraper sector and a few seconds later crossed many police patrols pursuing it.

The white letters of the Daedric Bank advertising hoarding reflected over the superbike pilot's helmet visor. That institution was the central bank of Black Earth. It was the most ancient, conventional, and towering building of the Pandemonical Continent. That edifice was black, static, and higher. It seemed like a fortress, which kept all Black Earth's treasures. It was a symbol of the entire orb's power and richness.

The sound of the requiem for Senator Malmo was in a crescendo, whilst at high velocity the superbike was leaving from city centre and approaching the congress. Suddenly, a transparent gel shield appeared surrounding both pilot and superbike. Police officers and soldiers opened fire, but the bullets stopped near that shield and then returned their way.

"*As upme*," the superbike pilot said with a robotic voice.

After pronouncing those words, that pilot and the superbike converted into black stardust. They were moving as fast as two dark grey clouds, whilst the soldiers and police officers were shooting at them. A white dove flew near a sniper that was pointing his weapon to the ameboid superbike pilot. A bullet fired by that shooter travelled the battlefield. The Requiem continued playing in ecstasy, whilst the bullet almost got the superbike pilot. The projectile could not reach its objective. Then, the terrorist and the superbike changed their stardust shape to regain its natural condition again. A soldier launched a rocket at them. It made the gel shield very fragile. However, the superbike pilot had arrived at Tartarusm Square. Then, that driver performed a big acrobatic jump. On air, that rebel held a small and powerful gun, which had a long-distance sight. Then, the superbike pilot shot a bullet, which was leaving two trails breaking the air frequency. The bullet went over people that were in the square.

A red-haired, blue-eyed, and white-faced kid was in front of Starlight's atrium. The kid left his pocket a souvenir. It was a snow globe of Befomet City, whose base had a name: Dubesor. Then, the kid offered it to Starlight. The senator's apprentice leaned to receive that gift. At that moment, the bullet triggered by the superbike pilot crashed into a transparent shielded screen. It was in front of Starlight's atrium at a considerable distance. Almost nobody noted that screen until a second bullet impact started fracturing that crystal. Instantly, security men fell on the young orator to safeguard him. Starlight's face appeared between those men.

"Protect the people!" he screamed holding the Dubesor with his right hand.

Meanwhile, a second rocket launched by a soldier broke the superbike pilot's gel shield completely. The pilot's helmet fell, crashing its visor against the pavement. Meanwhile, other bullets reached the superbike making it explode.

One of the military BESA helicopters was furrowing the blue-orange sky from Tartarusm Square to approach there. Suddenly, black fractal particles appeared orbiting in a spiral way making a hole behind the superbike pilot. That person had precious aquamarine eyes, pale face, and sun-bleached hair. She was a beautiful girl. The superbike pilot was the same water curtain silhouette (the Nymph). From her sensual scarlet lips escaped an orange monarch butterfly.

"Just for a while, I believed it was possible," she whispered.

Her body started mixing with the small black silhouettes behind her.

"*As upme*," she said to herself.

Suddenly, neither the Nymph nor the black silhouettes were there.

Starlight and his guards were a few blocks away from the Nymph's position. So, he could not distinguish his aggressor by the distance. Starlight just closed his blue eyes, and everything was obscured as in a winter night.

CHAPTER TWO

Teenage Rebel Minds

Black Earth was compounded by thirteen regions and each one had its own capital city. Sakopholus D'Moon City was the capital of Halocer (the region of the most splendorous sunsets). It was a modern city rounded by native woods and jungles. There, people dressed in summer clothes. In that city was a towering building with an angel shape in an upright position. Behind that stunning building, there were some dynamic skyscrapers, and a modern harbour. Sunrays passed through those constructions, sketching a light over the ocean. The wonderful weather of that region let the people have a natural and splendorous orange skin.

Mándala Heian Sun City was the capital of the Alucah Region. That capital was near a wonderful natural formation called Supreme Volcano. That city had modern buildings and big advertising hoardings on their roofs. At its city centre was its most emblematic construction, which was a dynamic crystal building with a cylindrical shape. It rotated over its vertical axis and at its top was a small castle. The ancient part of that city was surrounded by green, red, and yellow woods. There, people were dressed in majestic silky clothes. Their pretty slanted eyes denoted their lofty beauty.

Armeninov-Gord City was the capital of the Ahriman Region, which had many castles. They had architectural domes with the shape of coloured globes at their roofs. There, the snow covered all with its divine mantle. In that city, people dressed in big coats like Starlight's imperial jacket.

Blue-Ice City represented the capital of Ahvitchi (the fjords region). Near that city were the most beautiful cypress hills caressed by a dark blue ocean. Those hills were covered by the snow at their uppermost part. In one of those peaks was the governor's castle of that region. At the south of that city were small buildings of turquoise colour, with golden domes on their roofs. In that capital, the houses had beautiful window frames compounded by arcs with shapes of branches, flowers, and swans.

Agoras Classical City was the capital of the Dumah Region. Its constructions were near the shore. Its government buildings had immense columns, which ended in big chapiters. Two colossal statues were at the city entrance near the coast. They had helmets with wings on their heads and tunics that reached their feet. One of those sculptures hugged a book with its left arm, and the other one held a torch with its left hand. Both statues had their right hands making a stop signal. It meant people should think first about culture and illumination before accessing the city.

Pyramidal City was the capital of Eschem (the region of palms and deserts). That city had prominent constructions of ochre colour and big gardens. That place was in the middle of an oasis shaped by the Ur River. At the western-southside of that modern city were seven big pyramids pointed towards the Ophiuchus Constellation. People there had sculptural bodies of magnificent and wonderful cinnamon and black skin.

Hur-Appean Reich City was the capital of the Kheter Region. It was jammed of native woods and castles. In that city was an ancient gate compounded by high pilasters and antique chapiters. That construction had a mighty golden eagle with an inscription held by its claws:

In gott wir vertrauen.

People from that region had fair hair and green eyes, and most of the time the snow covered their precious curls.

Sanctus Imperium City was the capital of the Viechtisha Region. That city had a majestic building called the Templi Ominum Abba, which had a dome made of gold as its roof. There were wonderful constructions of white colour near the sea. There, people dressed in tunics as in Pyramidal City.

Golden City was the capital of Rofacaler, a quiet mountainous region. In that city were the most important bank headquarters of Black Earth. Those financial institutions were in a borough called Mological Block. A railway track crossed that city parallel towards a river called the Helvetica River. Golden City was compounded by cypress hills covered with constructions like little castles. People in that region dressed in black coats and leather gloves.

New-Light City was the capital of the Fleuretty Region. From the air, it was possible to see on that region the countryside and vineyards as a beautiful green patchwork-quilt. At its city centre, there was a square park and a massive tower made of bronze with an inscription on its base:

La ville du lumière.

People from that region were extremely elegant. They liked taking a cup of coffee and talking in luxurious cafés.

Sanct-Real City was in the Habraxas Region. That capital city had a monumental temple, called Black Earth Temple. On its roof, there was a big white dome. The temple was in front of the Square of Gods. That square had a rectangular obelisk at its centre. The architecture of that city was a mixture between ancient and modern constructions. Near the Square of Gods was Beliar Stadium. There, people played an ancient game: Eamun Disk. It consisted of a flying disk that must pass through a hoop at the top of a post. There was a hoop on two opposite sides of a rectangular field. Each one of those big loops was the shape of a golden snake biting its tail.

Be Alpha Men City was the capital of the Molog Region. That city was so charming. It had spacious parks and squares with many trees, monuments, and museums. The most prominent art galleries were at Memorial Pace-Park Avenue, which was the area of government buildings. In that city, there was a sculpture of General Be Alpha Men. It held on its right hand a sable and in the other one a book. The statue was on a plate, which had the following phrase:

The light of wisdom will give us this empire.

The last city of the thirteen regions was Befomet City, capital of the Netflimt Region. It was the most notable city of the Black Earth territories.

Few months had passed after the last attack against Starlight, and the election day for Congress President had arrived. In the Amon Room (the most important congress auditorium) were all the congressional representatives ready to vote. One hundred and one members compounded the congress (even the corporation president). Those representatives were the vox populi from the thirteen regions of Black Earth.

Congressional representatives spoke to each other, and the lobbyists were running. Moments later, the quorum majority had chosen. The new congress chairperson was Starlight by sixty-six votes. Thirty-two were neutrals and three against Starlight. It was the first time in all Congress history where one elected chairperson obtained more than fifty-one percent of the total voting in the first session.

The three senators that voted against Starlight were in disappointment with those results. They thought the elected Congress President was too young for that position.

Then, Starlight received congratulations from his sixty-six allies. In that congress room beautiful melodies of western transverse flutes started playing. People on the streets jumped with glee, and fireworks invaded the skies of each city in Black Earth. After congratulations and applause from congressional representatives and journalists' interviews, Starlight went alone towards Senator Malmo's office.

"It was worthwhile," he whispered.

The night had come, and Starlight was in that office looking through the window. Outside, the fireworks produced colourful explosions. Those lights illuminated his blue eyes.

The Nymph was in Tartarusm Square in front of Malmo's office building with many Befometians enjoying those wonderful sparklers. That spectacle seemed like a colourful rain of fire. There, people were cheering Starlight's name.

The Nymph had great cheerfulness, and her grins decorated her face. She was performing turns with her arms wide open. Suddenly, she appeared on a wonderful green grass field without explanation. That landscape had a blue-sky and mountains with their peaks covered by snow. The Nymph was smiling and then closed her precious aquamarine eyes and appeared in Tartarusm Square under the fireworks show again. She was seeing those fire explosions, whilst her eyes turned in a greenish colour.

Starlight continued looking at the crowd below when some feminine voices vibrated in the air.

"*Guten nacht.*"

He was searching for the source of those voices. Starlight turned his head and identified three beautiful teenage girls, who had entered that office.

"*Guten nacht, ich bin sehr froh für eure Anwesenheit. Können wir in der netflimtian, oder in kethererian sprache weitersprechen? Sie sind von Hur-Appean Reich City?*" Starlight asked them.

He wanted to know if they could speak in Ketherian or Netflimtian language. In addition, Starlight would want to clarify if those girls came from Hur-Appean Reich City by the language they were speaking.

Those girls were as poetry made flesh; their faces and bodies were like goddesses. One of them took the word. She had red hair, a white face, blue-sky eyes, and a gentle voice.

"My name is Aeda Cupida. It is so grateful to speak in the Netflimtian language for us, my Lord."

Another of those girls had grey eyes, and her hair was as black as the night.

"My Lord, my name is Meletea Vanety."

The third girl was very sensual like the other two. She was a youthful blonde. She had a white face and green eyes like grass on the ending spring.

"My Lord, my name is Nemea Mendacci."

"Oh well, now, I remember it. This meeting was on my master's agenda. It was scheduled a few months ago. My young ladies. What is the purpose of this pleasant visit?" Starlight requested them.

"We are representatives from Beliar High School and Royal Imperium University. Meletea and Nemea come from college and me from high school my Lord. The proposal of this visit is to inform you that all fraternities of our institutions are going to join in only one. We want to offer you our services from our research groups and our technology developments," Aeda answered him.

"Do you require financial aid in return?" Starlight asked.

"Only just the Law allows you, my Lord," Nemea said.

"Well, it is an interesting proposal. As a plant is irrigated with sunlight and water; education must be irrigated with investment, effort, and passion."

"We know about your exceptional achievements, my Lord. You have impressive scores and awards from Royal Imperium University and Beliar High School as well. You are an idol for the youth," Meletea said.

"I just did the right things at the right moment. That is all," Starlight said to them. Then, he giggled and continued.

"If you need resources, you are going to have them through education investment projects. All this in a legal way. Please, call the best people, students, scientists, athletes, and artists. We are going to be one."

"The Teenage Rebel Minds' House at your service, my Lord," the three girls answered.

At that moment, over Tartarusm Square occurred three big explosions in the sky. A dragon made of fireworks left each one of those blasts. They fell in three distinct trends growling like they were real creatures. Those fireworks crossed Tartarusm Square with their flashing wings opened over the people. A few moments later, those light dragons vanished in a tiny rain of multicoloured particles.

"Ketherus," the Nymph whispered, whilst she continued enjoying the show.

A few days later, a new afternoon had come. In the sky, a fighter passed furrowing the blue firmament. Suddenly, it executed a turn towards its right side flying so fast. Two military attack helicopters were flying near the fighter over Tartarusm Square. On the interior of those choppers, there were snipers pointing to the ground. In that square were the governors from the thirteen regions. Starlight would present his introductory speech as congress chairperson. Many people in that square were waiting for him with much glee.

Starlight left the Pandemonical Building kept by five guards who carried big guns and wore opaque spectacles. He was holding with his right hand the Dubesor. Many snipers were wakeful to any possible attack against Starlight. Mr Aroth was preparing the location for the new congress chairperson's speech.

"My Lord, the satellites are ready for transmission," he said to Starlight.

"I am ready Mr Aroth," Starlight replied to him smiling.

Starlight took the microphone, seeing the crowd.

"My people, time has been imposing on us proofs to maintain our peaceful life. Hence, we must clear the way to get the illumination and obtain the light. The gods offered us the understanding to determine the truth…"

At the same time in another location, the image of a blue planet reflected over an astronaut's helmet visor. That helmet had at its top part, holes for microphones and video cameras. The cosmonaut's dress of white colour had embroidered a BESA insignia on his right arm. A red pentagon and a black eagle compounded that symbol. The astronaut was attached at a communication station by a silver cord. He gave a turn so slowly over his vertical axis.

That BESA space station was called Toroid SGW-0023. Its name was given by its shape, and the initials meant Spatial Government Workspace. The exterior of the station had many solar cells and antennas. Its interior had many hologram screens hanging from the top of its inner white walls. Those artefacts projected information from government, military, and private television channels. That station had aluminium alloy doors and crystal windows, which showed a great view of a blue planet and its moon disks as well. Some shooting stars were decorating that panorama.

The astronaut started communicating with someone in that station.

"Here Alpha Hom can you hear me? Toroid SGW-0023, change."

"Here Toroid SGW-0023, clear and loud," someone from the station answered him.

"My visor instruments are failing."

"Possible cause Alpha?"

"An external magnetic field altered or recalibrated everything."

Far from the cosmonaut, was one spiral as a sink made of luminous clouds. Soon, that extraordinary phenomenon became a big circular light disk. From it left a ray towards the blue planet, which was called Sattrin Earth. It had a Pandemonical Continent subdivided in two parts: Black Earth and South Earth.

Then, the light disk exploded producing an enormous wave. It shook the astronaut making him give turns as decontrolled watch rods, whilst his silver cord moved so slowly.

"Mayday, mayday SGW-0023. Can you hear me?" the astronaut said with a fragile and nervous voice.

"Yes, Alpha Hom. Here SGW-0023. We are listening to some disturbance. What is happening?"

"I am observing an elevated electromagnetic field level on my instruments. I am giving turns, mayday, mayday."

"Well, we are going to retract the cord. Do not graduate up your mass body. The cord could break."

"I got it Toroid, but you must announce to BESA Headquarters that something entered Sattrin Earth. Roger."

The Toroid crew had the same white uniforms as the astronaut, and a BESA insignia embroidered on their arms as well. They were trying to understand the situation. That squad was watching Sattrin Earth on the hologram screens. A crewmember activated a small metal capsule. From it left three small, rigid, and thin cord lamps. Those cords produced a blue light, which reflected a few holograms screens and wireless keyboards. Some people of that crew had devices glued to their throats and ears as well. Those gadgets projected on hologram screens the crewmembers' voices as text and some of their thoughts as videos and pictures. An official girl who had brunette hair and blue eyes sent a hologram file from her mind to a computer making a beep. Near that official, there was a group of five captains rounding a crystal table. One of them had short blond hair and green eyes. He was Captain Thunder. Another official girl of blonde hair and dark brown eyes. She was holding a small ring. From it was projecting Sattrin Earth as a hologram. She got her hands on the hologram model of that planet. One of those officials broke the silence, whilst he touched his own short black hair with his right hand and opened his grey eyes. He looked at Captain Thunder.

"Sir, a kind of light is entering. It maintains a trend towards Befomet City."

Suddenly that light, which was travelling in a downwards way, converted into a luminous gargoyle. It had wings, extended legs, and eagle crows. It looked like a man with horns of brilliant golden colour as well.

Captain Thunder was watching that event on the spherical hologram. He took his ear microphone.

"Here Toroid SGW -0023, speaking Captain Thunder."

"Here Beta Persei," One officer with dusky brown eyes, a white face and black hair answered.

Beta Persei was at BESA Headquarters located at Be Alpha Men City, capital of the Molog Region.

"There is an unknown object entering Befomet City at 15,200 knots," Mr Thunder said.

"Specify Captain Thunder. Is it organic?"

"We do not know it yet," the captain answered.

Then, that Beta Persei officer took another microphone connected to other hologram screens, which showed different Pandemonical Continent locations.

"Red code, red code, alert on thirteen stations. Priority: The emperor's security."

Many small white, yellow, and turquoise butterflies started flying on a green field. There were satellite transmission antennas of white colour behind those small lepidopterans. That communication complex was rounded by a wind energy field. Those antennas had the BESA insignia and the name of Netflimt (the region where they were located). They rotated in a counterclockwise way towards the sky. In fact, each region of Black Earth had a similar complex.

A soldier with brown eyes and a precious black face was on the first deck of one of those Netflimt big antennas watching his hologram screen.

"Red code, red code, confirmed by BESA Headquarters," he said, taking his microphone.

Some soldiers started running over one of the landing runways in that military base, which was near the antennas and the wind energy field. Those militaries got on their BESA fighters.

The gargoyle that had entered Sattrin Earth continued descending from the sky. That monster was like a falling bolt of blazing gold.

"*Ny up, seed Morfim fee as not as,*" It said with a guttural voice.

Simultaneously, Starlight continued giving his speech on Tartarusm Square.

"…Do what thou wilt but do it with the light."

The angel-gargoyle was going downwards so fast. It was performing turns on its vertical axis with its head pointed down and its claws towards the sky. Above it, there were some clouds moving and the sun was revealing its pleasing face.

A premonition invaded Starlight. He remembered the instructions that he had given the military generals a few hours before his speech. …" In case of attack, send the drones first. I do not want my soldiers to be at high risk…"

He continued his speech when some drones of white colour furrowed the sky. They were ready to attack the angel-gargoyle. Those planes had splendorous big semi-delta wings, which had their pylons full of missiles ready to open fire. The drones shot at that creature with their torpedoes and submachine guns as well. The gargoyle was dodging those shootings. That beast had a spherical shield rounded it.

After many impacts from the drone's missiles, the monster's shield was broken. Its golden luminous body was a biomechanical armour, which burst into flames.

"*Ny up, seed Morfim fee as not as,*" that gargoyle said, whilst it fell.

Those words meant in ancient Nymphanian language: I am a Ny (Nymph), and I will release this burden.

At that point, the gargoyle left one sword from its destroyed armour. The monster continued saying.

"*Zen sheer naa wop yub loose am.*"

("Face the dead to live forever").

The gargoyle started breaking the torpedoes launched by the drones with its gleaming sword. The lean blade had a straight shape from its tip to its guard. That sword had a hilt of intertwined horses and swans at its pommel. The entire grip was of aquamarine colour and some rubies were embedded on its fuller. The gargoyle's armour vanished, and the blue-orange sky denoted a silhouette without its biomechanical cover. The body under that shell was an attractive juvenile girl. She had blonde hair like sunshine, a white face, eyes of aquamarine colour and a well-shapely body. Her semitransparent dress had embroidered flowers of golden colour and a long yellow fabric girdle, which was entangled on her forearms.

"*Temo febirt son hied hinga mieden him on hni,*"

("I do it for balance and righteousness").

she mentioned those Nymphanian words with her precious mouth.

One missile almost reached her, when she pronounced so weakly and crying another Nymphanian phrase.

"*As upme.*"

("Take me home").

Then, she vanished, and the missile continued its trend without reaching her.

The torpedoes' outbreak captured the attention of the people in the square.

A soldier gave an order, and the fireworks decorated the blue-orange afternoon sky. Those fires illuminated the heavens with explosions, which mixed with the last drones' shots.

Starlight raised his right arm holding the Dubesor.

"...Freedom and prosperity for all of Black Earth."

The fireworks furrowed the sky exploding and creating two intertwined swans, which started flying over Tartarusm Square. The drones were dodging those fireworks, making evasive manoeuvres. Below, people thought that it was an aerial exhibition.

Then, by the strongest noise of the pyrotechnical bursts, a flock of birds left behind a hill. Those small white passerines had picks of yellow and black colour. They were the Hur-Appean Ampelis, a wondrous kind of bird. Their tails were orange, and their heads were white.

Starlight was ending his speech.

"...inclusion for all people, education and transparency will lead our society. Thank you."

A roar of applause invaded the square. Mr Aroth, Aeda, Meletea, Nemea, some security guards, and a military general called Stealth approached Starlight.

The general was dressed in a grey coat, black leather trousers, and black boots. Tied at his waist was a broadsword with a snake shape at its pommel. The coat neck and fists of his clothes had snakes embroidered with golden threads. He had on his chest at the left side one rectangular band of red, black, and white colours. It represented the maximal distinction for any person who belonged to a military corp. Below that band were three gold medals. The first represented the moon in a waning crescent. The second was a five-pointed star and the last one was a circle compounded by two intertwined snakes.

Starlight was seeing that military man and giving him an accolade.

"General, I noticed the attack in the sky."

Those words surprised him, but the general tolerated that situation with serenity. That man had a beautiful cinnamon face and had his brown eyes fixed on Starlight. Slowly, that general touched his ear microphone with his right hand.

"Air clear."

Captain Thunder received that message in Toroid SGW-0023.

"Roger that, General Stealth."

"Everything is good, lads," Captain Thunder said looking at his aircrew.

Once the speech ended, everyone on Tartarusm Square went towards their homes. Starlight said goodbye to his friends and went to his limousine. He needed to rest.

On his limousine's path towards Royal Imperium University, he was thinking about a twist moving in three dimensions. Starlight was meditating, and then opened his blue eyes.

"Eureka."

"Pardon Sir?" The limousine driver inquired.

"Nothing fellow, I just was dancing with my mind."

Starlight's transportation arrived at the university guarded by five police motorcycles. He descended from that car looking at the dark night sky. There were few fireworks still on it.

Once on the campus, Starlight talked with some classmates and professors before entering his college residence building. Then, he came up the stairs and arrived at his room numbered three hundred and three. He was in front of his room door, which had one sophisticated and decorative security system. It consisted of a thin screen, which projected people in paintings. Those interactive personages allow people to enter rooms or deny the entrance.

"Good night, Mr Starlight," one of them said to him.

"Good night, Mr and Mrs Ranonilfi," Starlight replied.

Mrs Ranonilfi was dressed in a lemon green tunic. Under it, she wore a blue dress. She had a red belt made of silk below her big chest. On her head, there was a fabric piece of white colour. She had a white face, blue eyes, and brown horns. Her left hand was caressing her abdomen because she was pregnant. Mr Ranonilfi was dressed in a dark brown velvet tunic. He was holding the right hand of his wife. He had a big black hat on his head, which let us see his white face and green eyes. On a wall behind the couple in the image, there was a circular mirror with a wooden frame of an eight-pointed star shape. In the painting there was a golden candelabrum hanging from the roof. That chandelier was compounded by twelve candles, which were supported by twelve skulls and bones at their base.

"What about the baby?" Starlight asked them.

"Fine and growing so fast darling," Mrs Ranonilfi answered him.

Then, Mr and Mrs Ranonilfi let Starlight enter his room. It was eleven thirty-four at night. Starlight lay on his bed, closing his eyes. He turned off the lights of his room and all was obscurity.

Starlight almost fell asleep when he observed a small point of light on a wall. That bright glow expanded rapidly until blinding him. He tried standing up, but he could not move. His soul just rotated into his body. Starlight was listening to a mighty noise. That sound was like a mix of an enormous boat, tea kettles, and throaty voices. The walls of that room developed some distortion. His K-complex made little explosions in his brain. His body started ascending as a projection of a figure over a water mirror.

At the same time, the dust particles on the furnishings started ascending. It seemed like one anti-gravity field was acting there. Suddenly, all this chaos turned into a quiet view. At that point, Starlight opened his frightened blue eyes.

He was in a place jammed with shadows, amorphous figures, and dark green landscapes. The wind was blowing so hard. Far away, many thunders sounded, and some objects were falling while on fire. Starlight walked against the wind, trying to cover himself with his wonderful royal coat. It had embroidered small golden flowers and branches over his chest, lapel, and shoulders. Starlight had a black trouser and a knight's armour waistcoat made of thousand silver flakes. His hessian boots were made of dark-gold colour leather. There, a requiem was playing by a chorus of clear and gruff voices. They were singing in Nymphanian language.

"Ny up, seed Morfim fee as not as."
("I am a Nymph and will release this burden").
"Zen sheer naa wop yub loose am."
("Face the dead to live forever").
"Temofebirt son hied hingamieden him on hni."
("I do it for balance and righteousness").
"Him lihq not as him lihq not as."

("Follow the light to be free").

Starlight was in a gloomy wood. There was a park bank in that place. Therefore, he decided to sit down there. Then, he looked up and observed a red-orange sky. That location was a place with dark hills, dragons on fire, and where ghosts walked around randomly.

The sweet voice of a girl interrupted the chorus.

"Why did you betray me?" the melodic voice asked.

Starlight was scared and clung at that bank with his hands. He could not recognise that voice and its provenance.

"I never betrayed you," he answered.

"Do you love me?" the girl's voice interrogated him again.

"Always," a voice similar to Starlight's answered her, but he was not the person who responded.

So slowly, at his right side appeared a death-shadow. It had a long black rustic tunic. The shadow had pointed metal boots covered with a viscous black resin. That being had an intensive sulphurous odour. The mysterious ghost was faceless. It had armour gloves made of many metal flakes and a rough broadsword tied to its waist. That shadow walked leisurely, leaving a dark steam behind it. Starlight was frightened and felt as if an enormous external burden was exerting much pressure on his body.

His hands continued holding the black metal bank. The requiem chorus continued in an intense voice. Suddenly, from the empty head of that ghost appeared a silhouette of a skull. Then, it kissed the scared young.

This is the death shadow kiss. Starlight thought.

That ghost emitted a few deafening screams then went away from there so slowly.

Then, Starlight left his paralysis and observed his hands, which were elongating (as elastic gum). At that point, he jumped and arrived at another place. In that new location, there was a platform like a chessboard made of marble. Starlight started walking, his body felt so heavy. In fact, he broke a few tiles of that platform with his feet. The sky had the same red-orange colour, but it was not misty as before. Suddenly, the choral voices ended with a coda and silence filled that space.

There was a water drop hanging from a small bush. The drop fell, and its sound hitting the soil broke the quiet of that moment. In the background, there was a big grey tree moving. Soon, it transformed into a monster with many horns.

Just then, the chessboard plate was bending. The black squares of the platform were converted into window glasses of a building. The monster took Starlight by his left arm and launched him towards the glasses. Starlight crashed into those windows breaking them into a thousand parts. The crystal fragments leapt through the air. However, they stopped their trajectory, becoming windows again.

On the other side of those glasses, Starlight was in the middle of a red pyramid composed of many dead people and demons. He climbed on them to reach the pyramid top.

Much dark steam left each body, and the fog made it impossible to have a clear view of that sombre panorama.

CHAPTER THREE

The Sky Dancers

Starlight arrived at the pyramid top. There, he discovered a red reptile with bat wings. That monster was observing him with its yellow eyes. Starlight started a fight with that demon. He hit the creature with movements of martial arts. Meanwhile, a ray of light entered through a gel-window above them. Starlight arrived at that skylight and broke it. Then, he drew out his head over the gel surface and saw a kind of dirty toilet room. That gel was the content of a small pool. Starlight tried leaving from it but slipped and fell within that artificial pond three times. It was because the red winged reptile was pulling him. At the fourth time, Starlight left that pool. He was completely wet. Then, he sat down on the grey floor.

"Wow! Now, I comprehend what is born," Starlight whispered.

A dark steam was leaving from everything. That hideous place had two other lidos. They were filled with the same dark liquid mud.

Suddenly, two insects emerged from those pools. One was a big bug with a hard body and six legs (two largest at the rear and four smaller at its frontal part). It had a big horn on its head, two prominent antennae, and two small legs. It was a giant weta and had Starlight's feet size. The second insect was a tabanus, an enormous black horsefly. It flew from that pool directly to Starlight's back.

He screamed and pushed himself against a wall to try swat it. He just got the horsefly away from him, whilst the giant weta was creeping. Starlight was sliding because the floor and walls were wet. He could just hold himself from one dark goat head, which was hanging on the wall of that place. Starlight saw one dirty grey metal door, and then opened it.

At the other side, there was a sidereal space with dust clouds of light-purple colour and many shooting stars. Starlight saw an orb, which was between the Nergal and Eshudical-Sco Constellations. Near that planet, there were some brilliant stars and three moons in waning crescent. The light coming from the sun bent over the green planet's surface, creating a blue Aurora Borealis. There was a universal trigger in that magnificent universe. That colossal disk was formed when two dust masses collided with each one. From its centre, it could release at both sides a killing light as a pointer, able to destroy an entire galaxy.

Suddenly, a ray of light left the disk hitting the green planet. The explosion made the universe vibrate like a gel. Starlight perceived one immense column in flames, which rose from the impact zone. That pillar of fire was increasing its diameter each time whilst absorbing more material on its path. It seemed like an *Infernum Portam*.

One chorus was in the air singing in Nymphanian.

"Zen sheer naa wop yub loose am."

Starlight continued observing all that from the grey metal door.

Near the impact location, there was a fortress. That bastion had many rooms and passages in various underground levels. At its deepest level, there was a box of silver and gold colour with many figures hewn on its edges (intertwined snakes and lotus flowers). On the top of the box was hewn the figure of an owl with its wings opened, which was inscribed in a five-cornered star. The box was on a turquoise pedestal made of topaz and gold. There was a circle on the floor like a lotus flower beneath the pedestal. Many black and white bats formed it. There was a circle made of gold on the marble floor rounding that lotus flower. It contained the following inscription made of black gemstones:

Omnia est unum.

That golden circle on the floor was tangential to four marble columns. They had intertwined swans and at their topmost part and had demon heads as chapiters. The faces of those devils had not their noses, but they had big horns like rams. On the roof, there was an enormous gold spherical dome with hewn trees on its inner surface.

A big dragon-demon was keeping the box. That monster had a long dark body and bat wings. Its hands, arms, and legs were like a person. However, its feet were like eagle claws.

Then, a great sound made that place tremble with strength. The magma started entering there by the basal part. Starlight was amazed seeing that panorama, whilst the dragon burned rapidly giving a deafening screaming. Everything started breaking so fast by the fire. At that moment, the box was covered in magma. Then, that cubical container exploded, leaving a silver fluid as an eruption. The liquid traversed a considerable distance from that burning planet producing a great iridescent bright. Then, the silver fluid perambulated the outer space.

Starlight was observing that situation when a big sun was approaching him. He placed his left hand on his face covering his left eye from the shine.

Starlight locked the grey door of the toilet room of the three pools where he was. Unexpectedly, Starlight found hanging from the inner face of that door a grey pendulum clock. At its centre, there was a head of an owl inscribed in nine feathers. Some letters were rotating around that figure and stopped coining a phrase in Nymphanian language:

Zen sheer naa wop yub loose am.

Again, Starlight opened the door and found a green field instead of the magic parallel universe. Then, he entered that landscape.

In the background, there were some enormous dark pine trees. They were moving so slowly like the grass on soil and Starlight's clothes as well. Above the trees, there was a distorted reflex of the sun and a soft turquoise sky without clouds. There, the sunshine collided with the rustic wood of a park bank. It was covered by green mildew. The supports of that park bank were two dragons made of steel. They had enormous wings and three heads. Starlight was walking and then stopped for a moment to observe that park bank. Some seeds started elevating from the grass towards the heaven.

"This is my body," a femme voice said.

Suddenly, a shadow covered that delicate grass on the soil. An enormous whale shark flew so near Starlight. That whale had black and white spots on its dorsal part, and its pectoral was white. Its flukes and flippers were moving in a sinusoidal way. At that moment, Starlight noticed that he was not walking on the grass of a park. He was walking on the bottom of an ocean.

Starlight was scared and left escaping one air bubble from his mouth. Then, he started swimming upwards. He swam so fast to reach the water level surface. Starlight could just see the sun distortion and turquoise heaven. Once he achieved the sea level, the sun's reflection dazzled his eyes. Near there, a death-shadow was observing him.

"My Lord, my Lord," on air, some voices were saying.

Starlight listened to the sensual voices of Aeda, Meletea, and Nemea. He tried waking up and leaving from that nightmare and all those surreal visions.

The girls and Mr Aroth were outside of Starlight's room. They were requesting the security painting for permission to access the room.

Aeda was dressed in her high school uniform. It was composed of, one green mini skirt, one semitransparent white shirt and black leather boots until her knees. She wore her Beliar High School coat, which was black outside and green-blue plaid inside. On the left side of her coat, was the Beliar High School shield embroidered. It was composed by a golden inverted key of three circles as a bow. Below that shield was an inscription:

Ego caecusvos cum lux.

Meletea and Nemea were dressed in semitransparent dresses with arabesques. They had profound necklines embroidered with the golden forms of snowflakes and flowers, respectively. Their shoes were of ochre and dark turquoise colours. Their coats were of luxurious furs. Those girls had precious bracelets with jewels as diamonds and rubies as well.

Mr Aroth wore a luxurious formal black dress and a silk tie of the same colour. In addition, he had a long black coat and brown snakeskin boots.

Starlight's door opened abruptly. Then, Mr Aroth, and the girls entered.

"Please bring him a glass of water," Meletea said to Aeda.

"*D'accord,*" Aeda responded.

Mr Aroth got near Starlight, taking him in his arms. He noted both Starlight's sclera and iris had acquired a black colour.

"My Lord, art thou with me my Lord?" Mr Aroth asked, so scared.

At that moment, Aeda entered the room again. She brought the glass of water for Starlight. He drank a sip, but immediately he spat that water out. The three sensual girls looked at him with grace, whilst Starlight's eyes returned to his colour.

He was soaked in sweat.

Starlight said to his friends so weakly, "Loyalty remains a sophisticated light tool."

"Thank you, my Lord," Mr Aroth answered.

"At your service, my Lord," the girls replied.

The room was within complete disorder: books on the floor, broken mugs, and furnishings with scratches.

Starlight's eyes acquired pupils of a reptile and a black colour again. Meletea took her transparent handy phone and made a call. She called congress medical service.

"Mayday, mayday, code: one-zero-five. I repeat, we got a code one-zero-five. It is necessary air support. Our location is the Mological School at Royal Imperium University, the room is three hundred three. We need a medical assistant for Mr Starlight, the congress president. Please, come as soon as possible! Thank you."

At the other side of the call, was a man receiving it.

"We are going to go there. Thank you, my young lady."

He was a handsome doctor with curly hair, brown eyes, and a black face. Then, that man hung up the call.

"One-zero-five code at Imperium University, air support needed," he said to his medical team.

At that moment, Starlight's security corps were running. They entered the room and saw their chief in Mr Aroth's arms.

"Thank you, sirs. We need your help to take him to the hospital. A medical chopper is arriving," the sensual Nemea said to them.

The mighty dark heaven had a full moon, and the Nergal Bridge was its partner that night. Some Hur-Appean Ampelis crossed that sky. They were flying under the light of the moon and stars. The Gehenaesis River had its stream slow, but constant. It was describing a path of peace. On that river were reflecting the bridge, stars, and the streetlights. Soon, that peace was interrupted by tiny drops falling from the heavens. The rain broke the stream of the Gehenaesis River, sketching water waves into it. The rain got stronger, and the medical helicopter arrived at the campus.

The doctor and his team entered Starlight's college residence. Paramedics helped Starlight to lie on a stretcher. Security men and the doctor's team went in the chopper towards the hospital. Meanwhile, the girls and Mr. Aroth went in the limousine.

Near there, a little white butterfly was flying in a random way. It did so near a tiny water curtain, which fell from the Nergal Bridge. The silhouette of the Nymph was behind the water stele. She was seeing the path of the chopper and the black limousine with her aquamarine eyes. She had on a semitransparent long dress of a young empress with violet-blue flowers embroidered.

"I will see you soon."

A few days later Starlight left the hospital. He must assist at an important gala in one congress building. Starlight was the first person to arrive at that event. He walked along a corridor near a stair made of beige marble. That stair had balustrades in the shape of trees. The roof had a circular silver glass dome. The columns that supported the roof had architectural chapiters with bevelled flowers.

Starlight arrived at the second floor and listened to the music from cellos behind the principal wooden door. In front of that entrance, there were two guards dressed in formal attire. They had audio devices in their ears and mouths. Those minders were enjoying the odour of the pine polished from that door. They opened the gate for Starlight who was amazed observing that spacious and luxurious dining room. The tables had splendorous white tablecloths on them. They had on each lieu a white lamp. That dining room had big and high columns, which ended in arc wood trusses. From those arcs were hanging precious crystal lamps. They were compounded by candles with the shape of intertwined snakes. The windows located at sidewalls let enter the sunlight producing thousands of multicolour dust channels.

The central wall of that dining room had two paintings brought from the Habraxas Region. There, Starlight stopped his walking to see them. The first artwork was a painting of a blind girl. She had on her head a black bird feather, which was held by a purple diadem. She was dressed in a green tunic and a blue and golden scarf. That girl was touching her chest.

The second painting had a blue-sky with some clouds and small flying objects in the air in a city with a beacon. In that composition, there was a cart pulled by two ocelots. They had their heads as wolves. An angel without wings was on that cart. The angel had a white face, black hair, and blue eyes. That being just wore a big red flannel. There was a girl talking with that angel. Behind the cart were two demons trying to capture some maidens.

The guests started arriving at the gala. The television channels of Black Earth were in that place. A few moments later, that dining room was full of people, great dignitaries, politicians, the governors from the thirteen regions with their respective delegations, and journalists. All of them would enjoy the great banquet. The food of that feast was compounded by beef, fish, shrimps, red and white wine. In addition, it had many salads, desserts, and ice creams. The cutlery was made of gold as in Beliar High School and Royal Imperium University.

A half hour later, the music from the cellos stopped playing. The doors of the principal entrance of that dining room opened again slowly. Three knights entered there. They had turquoise metal armours and silver broadswords fastened at their waists. Their white faces were uncovered. One of those knights left a golden bugle called the Lebrags Bugle, and he made it sound.

"Your Majesty, the emperor," another knight said.

At a slow pace, a well-shapely masculine body entered that dining room. The emperor was dressed in a golden armour and high boots until his knees. He had a vest made of thousands of small gold rings, and its centre had a plate with an embossing eye. In addition, he had a turquoise silk cape on his back and a helmet made of gold. It had slots for his eyes and some holes for breathing.

The emperor walked greeting everyone with his right hand, whilst each one there made him a reverence. He walked through the dining room. He stood behind the main table, which was in front of the two Habraxian paintings. The emperor took the fourth chair at that principal table, which had seven seats. That allocation let him see all the people in that room.

He raised his right hand, and everyone was silent. The emperor started giving a short speech.

"My fellows. Today is a memorable day. The youth and knowledge of the universe had joined in this talented boy whose name is Starlight. He has shown us that constancy, righteousness, and will are the most powerful arms to preserve and guide our society. Congratulations

Mr Starlight to be the youngest congress chairperson in Black Earth's history. In the following days, he will graduate with honours from our prestigious institution, Royal Imperium University."

Everyone acclaimed him in a stand-up position. Then, people sat down, and the music and dining continued.

At the right side of the emperor were Starlight, Nemea, and Aeda. Mr Aroth, Meletea and General Stealth were at the left side of the emperor. Those seven personalities were talking about various themes like politics and economics. On the base of that big table, there was a hewn figure of a reptile head. It was camouflaged with the texture and colour of the dark wood table.

The emperor looked at Starlight.

"Son, you are the chosen one. Heretofore and beyond your behaviour must evince that you are a faithful friend of the Hur-Appeans. You must help guide our congress. In case of war, sickness, or poorness, you will defend our land with your blood. You will not let alone our people. You will not let them perish in hunger, cold, or nakedness. This time is yours, Starlight master of the universe," he said to Starlight with a profound voice.

"I will not be less than that, sir. In this shrine, I accepted the duty to lead both our people and the peace of the universe. This noble fact is on my mind so focused. I will defend all the ancient principles of my race," Starlight replied to him.

"So be it. Young Starlight, I heard from some congress representatives that you are going to take aerial military training."

"Yes, your Majesty. I am going to start tomorrow."

"That is interesting news."

The gala continued and everyone enjoyed that night.

On the next day, a black limousine arrived at the Befomet City military airport. Some technicians were checking the wheels and fuselage of the fighters in the hangars. At that moment, Starlight descended from the black limousine. There, a brunette military officer was waiting for him. Her uniform had the BESA insignia embroidered on her left sleeve, and the Black Earth flag was embellishing her right sleeve. The last name of that girl was Flussman. She gazed at Starlight and made him a smile and a bow.

"Officer Flussman at your service, my Lord. Nice to meet you. I am going to be your trainer. It is time for your first fighter training."

"Nice to meet you as well. My name is Starlight, and I am ready for the action. My young lady. I believe your training would help me dance in the sky."

"Sky dancers my Lord. That is a great honour for me."

Meanwhile, they were speaking, two fighters decorated that blue-sky with two red steles making a big x-letter in the sky.

Then, Starlight went to change his clothes. For the first time, he was dressed in a pilot uniform. He was walking at the right side of Officer Flussman. She was seeing him in a lovely way. Behind them, there were air distortions produced by an exhaust heat of a fighter.

Starlight and the beautiful military pilot got into a double cabin fighter. At that point, a technician removed the steel stair from the right side of that plane. She lifted down her sun visor and the fighter canopy as well. Starlight was behind her in the second pilot position. He had his eyes so opened. Starlight had much anxiety about his first military flight.

The plane started rolling on the runway. That fighter had an anhedral wing body seen from its frontal view, and a swept wing seen from its superior view. The plane was flying with the big orange sun of the morning as the background and downwards the green mountains. At the same time, a flock of birds (Hur-Appean Ampelis) furrowed the sky.

"My Lord, now the plump bird is in your hands. Show me what you got," Officer Flussman said to Starlight putting the combat plane in a horizontal position.

"Here we go," Starlight replied to her holding his fighter control stick.

Starlight was so nervous. His plane went into a tailspin, and he started elevating upwards as in an anti-gravitational field. However, he took the stick located in front of him again. Starlight got to stabilize the plane. Then, he started moving the stick from the left towards the right.

"Time is so curved my young lady," Starlight said to his flying instructor.

"Well done my Lord, go on like this," Officer Flussman said to him, whilst clouds were moving upon them.

Day by day, Starlight continued taking more pilot and personal defence lessons given by lovely Officer Flussman. In the same way, months passed so fast.

One morning, Starlight was in front of a Death Angel again. He had reached the minimum number of classes to pilot a military combat plane by himself. Once on his fighter, Starlight lifted down his helmet visor. On flight, he started making great manoeuvres. He did a turn of one hundred and eighty degrees in the air like a loop and some stratocumulus moving rapidly. Once Starlight landed, he felt so happy to have had that experience.

That afternoon after his flight, Starlight was in a congress plenary giving one speech in the Amon Room. That auditorium was divided into three big areas forming a circular sector. The room had on the topmost part of its walls many big convex hologram screens. Those screens were transmitting three-dimensional images.

All congressional representative's chairs were made of burgundy leather. On each of their desks, they had their names inscribed on a white plate. In front of them there was a big rectangular golden wall and from its centre was hanging a huge security painting. It represented a semi-naked woman, walking on dead people in a city in flames and bearing a Black Earth flag. At her left side there was a boy holding two guns, one in each hand. His right gun was pointed towards the sky and the other one in the direction of the soil. That poor boy wore a haversack of white colour with a reptile insignia on it.

Starlight was on the podium in front of the auditorium and started his speech.

"What is happiness, a feeling or state of mind? The virtuousness of happiness is the product of the interrelation between many elements of society: security, economic growth, job opportunities, health, education, and peace. We are not here to govern ourselves. We are hither to represent the voice of our people…" The energy of Starlight continued in crescendo. "The corruption infects society as a pestilence. We must transform that fact, investing more in sciences, arts, education, and researching. This is the moment to give a jump to reach a new universe, to get a modern mind conscience. Our duty is to prepare us now for the future, for us and our emerging generations. Thank you."

CHAPTER FOUR

The Rhapsody of Mind

Starlight dedicated his time in the mornings to speak in congress sessions in favour of the underprivileged and oppressed people. In parallel, he gave conferences about different social themes as well. At nights, he supervised technological projects of research groups from Beliar High School and Royal Imperium University. In the afternoons, Starlight went to give instructions to some research groups in the college. There, he started talking about dynamic fluids. Suddenly, he noted that Officer Flussman was in one of those laboratory groups. She was setting up a wind tunnel. She put into it a strange scale model of a white spaceship with a dragonfly shape.

"My Lord, we have problems with the bending of light," Officer Flussman said to him.

"I am going to show you the real meaning of bending light," Starlight replied.

He walked towards the wind tunnel, which was composed of a big translucent crystal box filled with transparent oil. An inner device allowed entering ink into that glass cube. Starlight and all his apprentices were standing up in front of that box.

"Look at my appearance on this crystal surface. From this position, it is normal. If I give one step backwards, my image starts deforming. Now, if I am getting closer to the container, my appearance is inverted. It is the same basic theory of plane mirrors. In this way, I bend myself like a spoon. Light got bent near me. The effect of the twisting body is given by the light and not by the body per se," Starlight said to her.

"My Lord, you have clarified my thoughts," Officer Flussman said to him, amazed.

"Do not forget the principles of the flux transportation equations, and the models into the wind tunnel. We can fix the spread of non-visible fluids that compound the universe," Starlight said to all groups there.

Another handsome young man with slanted eyes made some adjustments on his group project based on Starlight's words. Suddenly, a device with two poles generated a light from flowing iron filings. That flow generated a luminous sphere, which started giving turns creating a reptile eye. It was looking everywhere. That eye had a sclera of green colour and a black elongated iris. All people from other research groups applauded.

At the end of that laboratory session when that room was empty, Officer Flussman approached Starlight and said to him, "It seemed yesterday when you descended from the fighter in the first session. You were green and vomited on the pavement. Now my Lord, it is an honour for me that you teach me about hydraulics themes."

At that moment, Starlight remembered that scene. He descended from the fighter and vomited some transparent tadpoles.

"Yes, my young lady. It was so funny and nasty as well," he said to her with happiness on his face.

"Although, my Lord. Were you scared?"

"Horrified, frightened, paralysed … by you."

"At least my Lord, you reached up into the sky," she said to him, smiling.

He smiled as well. Then, they left the laboratory.

At noon of the following day, Starlight was in front of the congress plenary in the Amon Room. He would give a new speech and his powerful voice started declaiming it.

"The rise of the interest rates by the central bank would be a serious mistake. Higher rates make it difficult to pay financial obligations. The underprivileged people will not have the possibility to get credit. Higher rates control the inflation, but they constrain the capital flow. That mechanism just helps to grow the financial system, but not the whole economy."

Some senators murmured and made disapproval gestures.

Starlight continued, "Elevated rates stop the production system and let the financial sector grow by selling package debts. Those sophisticated financial instruments are the massive destruction weapons for the people. Those packages will rise as bubbles until the maximum speculation. At that point, their prices will fall until zero value. It will be an absolute catastrophe for all sectors, even the financial itself."

One of the three congressional representatives that had not voted for Starlight as congress chairperson, got up from his seat. He was a fat, old, white faced, and blue eyed man. That representative was dressed in a black formal dress: a white shirt and a blue tie. He looked at Starlight.

"Son, your inexperience here is so obvious. You do not know anything about banking, Mr Starlight. I have thirty-three years of experience, which is more than your whole age," the senator said to him with a sneer.

"Estimated Senator Thade, here your experience is not relevant because you had made the wrong things for thirty-three years. That situation is not to be proud of anything. Sir, my age is different from yours, it is true. However, I have the certified knowledge to make the right macroeconomics decisions. You must remember, I obtained the *Egregia Cum Laude* in economics program from the Mological School of Economics. That academic institution did not accept you because of your low records in your high school," Starlight replied to him.

"Egricum Laurenth? What is that? A new religion? Please, you must focus on the relevant themes, little boy," the senator said to Starlight with a sneer again.

Another senator in the Amon Room, an elegant and pretty black woman took her microphone. She replied to the fat representative, "It is not a religion, Senator Thade. It is the highest-level distinction for an academic degree, *Egregia Cum Laude*. You fool."

Starlight took the word again. "Estimated representatives, will you approve the Regulatory Law of the Bank Rate Intermediation?"

The hologram screens above the semi-naked dressed woman security painting were projecting the results of the voting. There were seventy-seven votes in favour of that law, twenty-one neutrals and three against it. Most of the congressional representatives rose to applaud Starlight, except the three senators opponents

to Starlight's policies (Messrs, Thade, Raw, and Paulge). Some members of Daedric Bank made gestures of resignation and anger due to the approved policy.

Senator Paulge was an old man. His hair was red, and his face white. He took his microphone and said to Starlight, "You will lead us to a black hole."

Starlight gazed at that old politician and said to him in ancient Leviathan language, *"Lupus est homo homini."*

Then, the young Congress President continued speaking with a strong voice looking at the entire auditorium.

"The wisdom over the force will return the light of the Empire to us."

After that speech, Starlight left the congress and went towards the university. Once there, the wind stroked gently against some Hur-Appean Ampelis, which were flying under that afternoon blue-sky over a green field at the Mological School of Economics. Starlight was in that place with his friends: Aeda Cupida, Meletea Vanety, Nemea Mendacci, Mr Aroth, General Stealth, and Officer

Flussman. They were seeing some advances in different research projects from Beliar High School and Royal Imperium University financed by the congress.

One of those developments was the spider dress, named in honour of the black widow. That polymer clothing had a black colour. It would let people walk on the water and give jumps like parkour. At that moment, five young people wore spider dresses.

A girl of those teens jumped climbing a wall giving turns in the air. It seemed like she was dancing. Another teenager ran on the roof of the Mological School building. He jumped a high lamppost of black colour and an arc shape decorated with steel flowers at its upper end. Then, he descended by that vertical streetlight. Another young girl was running and gave a jump reaching the half of a small column at the back entrance of the Mological School building. She gave a second jump and hung from the second deck. There, her body bent like a scorpion, and she got standing on the balustrades of that deck. Another young man touched a lamppost with his two hands and started climbing it completely perpendicular towards the rod. The last teenager of that group started running on the roof of Mological School as well. Behind her was a lovely sun and a few white stratocumuli. Some Hur-Appean Ampelis were flying there. Then, she executed a turn in the air making a mortal jump in a counterclockwise way. That attractive blonde girl continued jumping until reach the floor. In that place was located a pool with a blue fluid.

Once she landed there, started walking on that fluid as a basilisk lizard.

"My Lord, everything is splendorous. What is the idea with all these?" General Stealth asked.

"General, do you remember the Luftbeat files? A strange silver fluid, which travelled through the immense darkness of the universe. So, that liquid crossed the asteroid belt to enter Sattrin Earth. Once on this planet, that fluid fell like a fire rain in the sky. That drizzle was falling over the lovely conifers of the Ahvitchi Region, on Eschem Region desert and Halocer Region volcanoes. Its drops were an effluvium, which had a viscosity like soft gel. So, well. We collected an amount of those cosmic parts. We treated it in our laboratories in Beliar High School and Royal Imperium University."

"So, my Lord. All this innovative technology is based on that gel?" General Stealth asked.

"Yes, my friend."

"Although, it's not entirely clear for me. How could a cosmic gel lead a technological change?"

"My friend, the gel was treated at uncommon temperatures. In an amazing way. The fluid changed its chemical and physical properties at each temperature, passing from metal towards polymer."

"Metal and polymer? So, that means that such material could be used in weapons?"

"Yes, in fact, there are more developments to be done."

Starlight made a sign with his right hand and all members of those research groups stopped the exhibition.

"My friends, thank you for making this dream possible," he said to them with a strong voice.

The security personnel helped each research group to carry on their projects towards the hangars of Beliar High School and Imperium University. General Stealth was so happy with those technological advances and all new ideas.

"General, we must meet later to talk about these themes," Starlight said.

"Yes, my Lord."

The night started covering the students' buildings of the Imperium University. Starlight and his friends after the exhibition went towards their homes. Once the congress chairperson arrived at his college room, he remembered a personal defence class taken by him. That was a fencing class imparted by Officer Flussman. That girl was dressed in a white fencing uniform, whilst Starlight had a black one.

They took their positions, one in front of the other. Their breathings were slow, and their minds were very concentrated. Their harnesses were attached to their backs. Their charming eyes were looking at themselves behind those black face protectors. A horn sounded, and the first step was given by Starlight. Officer Flussman's fencing broadsword cut the air horizontally and Starlight gave a great jump. He was suspended in the air as if he was a hummingbird. Then, Starlight with his broadsword made a touché on Flussman's chest. The muscles of those competitors were moving like waves with each fencing movement.

Starlight shocked his sword against the floor and some micro fragments of metal left his blade. Those pieces were flying towards Starlight's right eye and then entered there. Those silver particles arrived at his blood stream. They went through his veins towards his brain. There, those metal fragments exploded like a supernova, forming chains of green DNA. That spectacular collision in Starlight's brain was converted into a magnificent show of fireworks. Suddenly, Starlight's eyes transformed into black reptile pupils. Then, in one magical attack, he won that fencing match against Miss Flussman. Finally, Starlight smiled by remembering that episode and then got to sleep on his bed.

The next day, Starlight was looking through the window of his black limousine at the blue-sky. He saw some wonderful cypresses as well. He was taking his path from the university towards congress. That would be the last time of that journey because in a few days, Starlight would receive his new home residence in one area near the congress.

On the campus, a grass-green butterfly was flying in a leptokurtic path, and it arrived at a field formed by thousands of sunflowers. On its trend, that butterfly was leaving some drops of water, like a tiny stardust. Near the little green butterfly was the Nymph.

She had on a semitransparent dress with golden flowers embroidering, and a diadem made of gold. Her shoes were decorated with many roses made of golden threads. She was seeing Starlight's black limousine and his motorcycle guards. He was observing her as well. Starlight gave an order to his driver to stop the limo. Then, he descended from the car as a king from his noble steed. Starlight wore a coat of beige colour with details of flowers and branches embroidered in golden threads as well.

The wind took away some Taraxacum Officinale seeds towards a black and red tree. Its colour was given by a big swarm of ladybugs. They left flying with the wind, and that tree obtained its own greenish vestment again. The ladybugs flew on the Taraxacum seeds as witches flew on their brooms.

The Nymph and Starlight had drawn a smile on their faces. She made a sign with her left hand to greet Starlight. Her middle and ring finger pointed downwards and the index and little finger upwards. The congress chairperson made the same sign. Starlight was approaching her, stepping one branch unexpectedly. At that moment, some yellow birds started flying.

"I know your face, my young lady. The image of your beauty is still bending my thoughts," Starlight said to her.

"My Lord, I am glad to see you again. My name is Lilith."

"Beautiful princess... where are you from?" Starlight held her right hand.

"I come from the stars like you, my Lord. I come from nothing and everything at the same time," she answered him.

"You have not answered my question yet," Starlight interrupted her.

"My Lord, I come from the place that has the prettiest view of fjords."

"Interesting, you come from the Ahvitchi Region where the fjords are part of the universe's magnificence."

"If you say it my Lord, so be it."

Starlight guards were seeing them, whilst the yellow birds continued flying there.

He said to Lilith, "I feel happy when I am near you. Your glamour overshadows the firmament due to you being the beauty itself."

Lilith was looking at Starlight with her big green eyes. "Pretty words, my Lord. I thought that you must say the same things to every pretty girl that you meet everywhere."

"My lady, that was a little offensive to me. I just want to express to you, my thoughts. Now, I feel a little bit awkward about all this. I would like to leave with alacrity from this situation."

"My Lord, I am a simple city centre girl. Everyone believes in this world that I am a princess, but that is untrue."

"The truth is just an invented lie," Starlight smiled and said to her.

At that moment, a wave of air rounded them. Some ladybugs continued flying over the Taraxacum Officinale seeds.

"This is an eternal moment. My Lord, do not you think so?" Lilith asked him.

"Any eternal moment with you is now," Starlight said to her.

She looked at him and held his right hand. "I just want to enjoy this precious moment with you for eternity. In two weeks, I am going to travel towards Blue-Ice City. The governor's castle is my house, and I hope you see you there my Lord."

That couple was walking towards the limousine. Then, Starlight and Lilith said goodbye. He gave her a kiss on each cheek, and both gave themselves a large hug. Starlight and his security scheme returned towards the diplomatic car again. The congress chairperson would give a speech about genetic research in the Amon Room. He had enough time to arrive at that place.

A luxurious bulb light illuminated one spacious room of the congress. In that place, there were silhouettes of three men settled in three golden chairs decorated with many trimmings. One of those men had a large dark wooden cane with a golden snake handle. That man was Senator Thade, who faced Starlight on the voting day of the Bank Rate Intermediation Law. At his right was Senator Raw, who had a fat figure and green eyes. He had another wooden cane with a golden bird handle. At his right was Senator Paulge, who had a golden owl as a cane handle.

"The plan is as he wants. All is on its course," Senator Thade said.

"What if the plan fails? The purity of the transition will be cut?" Senator Raw replied.

"No, my friend, he did the plan. Therefore, it will be perfect," Senator Paulge said.

"Yes, he will do it as sadistically and slowly as the same gods will do it," Senator Thade added.

Then, the three men let sketched giggles from their faces.

Once Starlight arrived at Amon Room, he stood in front of the congressional representatives who were there. He started giving his speech with a strong and powerful voice.

"The stench of ignorance constitutes the principal reason for a country suffering the consequences of underdevelopment. Today, we have in our hands the possibility to recognise more about ourselves than never. The cryobiology project represents our future in the present. It gives us now the possibility to create new discoveries to benefit our lives. Welcome to the concept of a flourishing life. Welcome to the rhapsody of the mind…"

Meanwhile, Lilith had arrived at one ancient edifice of the university after the casual meeting with Starlight. She opened a door with a golden key and entered a laboratory. That girl was walking between some crystal crypts. Suddenly, Lilith felt something warm descending by her nose. A bit of her precious green blood was flowing down over her sensual red lips. She cleaned it with her white embroidered handkerchief. Lilith touched those crypts, whilst she was walking and seeing straight forward with her precious aquamarine eyes.

Starlight was ending his speech. "...Those themes gave us a great advance in health problem solutions. Thank you."

Mr Aroth approached him and started to talk, whilst they walked towards the back door of the Amon Room.

"Mr Aroth, we are going to go towards Blue-Ice City, capital of the Ahvitch Region," Starlight said to him.

"Why, my Lord?" Mr Aroth replied.

"My friend, I need to set up the Pandemonical Integration Project."

"My Lord, I am going to prepare everything related to your trip. However, the congress is unvoted for that program yet."

"The union and peace represent the principal arguments for this task, which is the base to create a real civilised society."

"The union of a society is one contract made by many parts and not by just one. Regardless, everything is susceptible to change."

"So be it my friend."

They left the congress to take a rest in their houses.

The next day, Starlight, Mr Aroth, and the girls were arriving at the train station of Befomet City. People were greeting Starlight as a celebrity, and he answered them in a gentle way.

Nemea approached him wearing an elegant dress of beige colour embroidered with red flowers. She had on a semitransparent cardigan of rose colour. Behind her, many people were walking under the morning golden sky. Aeda was walking wearing a precious soft-blue dress, and Meletea ported another dress of lilac colour.

"My Lord, we are here as you requested us," Meletea said.

Aeda was a little worried.

"Why are we going to travel by train? My Lord, is it not risky due to the last situations?" she asked.

"You do not you worry about it. We have enough security personnel during the travel," Starlight answered her while smiling.

"Well, if you said it, so be it. My Lord, we must move fast, or we will miss the train," Nemea said.

The girls and Starlight started running behind the train like children.

"Why are we running?" Nemea asked Starlight.

"Because we must not forget the happiness of life," Starlight answered her.

Those friends were enjoying all that together because they have almost the same age range. Some of Starlight's guards were running behind them as well. At that moment, a white commercial plane was flying above the station in an ascending and diagonal way decorating the sky.

On the train, Starlight and his friends were walking through a corridor trying to find their chairs. That was not a commercial travel, the entire train was reserved by the government for Starlight, his diplomatic, and security staff. That classic train model had a silver colour. The lateral sides of the locomotive and coaches were decorated with a big scarlet red stripe, whose upper and lower borders had black colour. The locomotive had written the name Surut in white letters between the frontal square headlamps. Over the train were flying two military attack helicopters, which were part of Starlight's security.

CHAPTER FIVE

The Train Window

The interior of that coach train was so cosy. It had walls of dark wood, and green leather sofas allocated near windows. In addition, there were curtains of small squares of ochre, red, and olive colours. Starlight and his friends were talking there.

"My Lord, I am worried about your safety," Nemea said to Starlight.

At the same moment, Aeda and Meletea agreed.

"My ladies, you do not worry. We are going to Blue-Ice City. I have a rendezvous with Princess Lilith…" Starlight answered them.

"Who?" at the same time, the three girls interrupted him.

Starlight looked at them with his blue eyes in a tender way.

"I am going to get peace and unification between Black Earth and South Earth. Then, I am going to travel towards South Earth to talk with the supreme leader of that part of our continent. For that purpose, I am going to convince the leaders of each Black Earth region to get their diplomatic support."

At that moment, the happiness of the beautiful young girls became sadness.

"The Agnesii are our enemies and are wildering and hostile. My Lord, that is a risky enterprise to do," Aeda with tears in her eyes said to Starlight.

Nemea gazed at Starlight with her green eyes.

"My Lord, we suppose they are the authors of the attacks against you."

Meletea opened so wide her grey eyes.

"*Mein Herr, willst du sterben und uns allein lassen?*"

"*Nein!! Ich…* no, Lady Meletea. I am not going to die or leave behind any of you, my friends. I just want to bring to this universe another kind of life. I want to get peace and justice for all. No more divisions! No more fears! I want to find a political solution for a new and prosperous society," Starlight answered.

"If you really desire it, we are with you, my Lord," Meletea said to him.

"Yes, my Lord, we are with you," Mr Aroth replied as well.

"Good, so we are going to eat some chocolates," Starlight said to them.

"My Lord, I believe you just want to eat chocolates when you are under pressure," Meletea added.

"There is always space and time for chocolates," Starlight answered her, and all made giggles.

At that moment, a man appeared there. He came from the train service coach.

"Good morning, ladies, and my lords. My name is Rainman, and I am making the checks for the tickets. Aeda Cupida please?"

"Here sir," The red-haired, white faced, blue-sky eyes girl answered.

"Thank you, Lady Aeda. Now, Meletea Vanety?"

"Here sir," The black-haired, grey eyes, and the same Starlight's age girl, answered.

"Finally, the sweet blonde is Nemea Mendacci, right?" the elderly and amiable man asked.

"Yes, I am at your service, sir." the young blonde girl of green eyes answered him with a giggle on her face.

"Oh, thank you. It is a great honour to meet each one of you. I am here to serve you, princesses, and my lords as well. In fact, I heard that you need chocolates. I am going to bring you the most delicious chocolates from the Rofacaler Region. They were elaborated in Golden City," the friendly man said to them, smiling.

"Thank you," Starlight responded to him.

At that point, the old man left Starlight's coach to bring them the cocoa bars. Then, Meletea took the word again.

"So, my Lord. Who is Lilith?"

"Oh yes, she is the princess from fjords Region," Starlight answered her.

"Why are you going there first? It is the westernmost side of Black Earth, my Lord. Why do not we start from the eastern of the continent? The Ahriman Region, for example?" Meletea asked.

"Or the Molog Region?" Nemea asked as well.

"Do you have any interest in the Ahvichi Region? In the new princess that we do not know yet. We just want to know it for your security, my Lord?" Aeda inquired.

"First, these are political decisions focused on the peace of our society. Second, you are my friends and not journalists trying to analyse my answers," Starlight responded vehemently.

"My ladies, he knows so well what he is making," Mr Aroth said to the girls.

"We just do not desire more events that put your life at risk, my Lord. We are at your service," Nemea said.

"We are at your service, my Lord," The other two girls said.

"Well, as everything is clear we are going to enjoy the chocolates. I can see Mr Rainman approaching again," Starlight said to them.

Then, they talked more about Lilith and different themes as well.

The train was still leaving from the Netflimt Region to enter the Fleuretty Region. There were wonderful lilacs and green flowers on the grass, vineyards and hills covered by cypresses. The train passed so fast along a bridge. Behind it, there was a big fall formed by a precious lake. The bridge had at its bottom part arc shapes, and trusses of beige colour at its uppermost part.

Meanwhile, in one alleyway near the Memorial Pace-Park Avenue, at Be Alpha Men City (capital of the Molog Region); a small cloud of dust made a twist of air.

Suddenly, that wind spiral became black particles, which moved in circles. From there, Lilith appeared dressed in black leather clothes and two young men were with her as well. Those men had white faces, blue eyes, and long fair hair dressed in the same manner as Lilith.

That group stole a big black sport utility vehicle, which was parked there. The car had big wheels and a silver front grill. Lilith was driving very fast in that stolen car when some police patrols started pursuing them.

On the auto, Lilith got a broadsword from a bag of one of her companions. That blade had a snake hewn on its pommel. Lilith broke the floor of the car making a circle with the broadsword. The group left through that gap, whilst officers from the patrols were shooting at that sports utility car. Then, the vehicle left the driveway and broke the balustrades of a little bridge, falling directly towards one river. The car was hit by a shot from the police and then exploded in the air. Meanwhile, the three rebels were diving in the river trying to reach some inner drainage tube. They beard electronic devices in their mouths to breathe.

Near there, a red-haired and grey-eyed teenage girl was walking in front of Beta Persei Complex. She dressed in black leather clothes. Many white, yellow, and turquoise butterflies were flying over a green field behind the security fence of that complex. It divided the street and the satellite transmission antennas area. Those white antennas had parabolic form. The BESA insignia and the name of Molog were painted on them. The red-haired teenager continued walking there, when she left an electronic device like a phone in one trash can. The guards of the complex did not notice what the girl was doing. Those soldiers were so concentrated watching Lilith's pursuit on television. The red-haired teenager continued her way, whilst the wind was caressing her white and precious face.

Minutes later, the three fugitives had arrived at an underground drainage system. They left wet from a big tube and started synchronising little electronic devices to glue them against the walls of that subterraneous deck. Then, those rebels arrived at a metal stair, which was under a steel drainage lid. They climbed the stairs and left there finding a wonderful green garden, which was in Beta Persei Complex.

"*D'accord,* this is the moment. There is so much to win, so please be careful. We already charge the explosives below. Now, we are going to proceed according to the plan. Graduate your micro panel dresses to get the invisibility. Then, put your spectacles for radiation emission and calibrate them at a beta-gamma synchronisation of eighteen mili-rems. In this way, we can see ourselves. My friends remember, we have an external distraction. It will help us," Lilith said.

They obtained from their bags the black night vision spectacles. The fugitives put them on and then pressed a button on their dresses. Their clothes changed the polymer fabric appearance. They became invisible because thousands of micro video cameras were connected to their dresses. Those devices recorded in real time the rear images and then projected them at the frontal part of each one of their dresses and vice versa. Then, the intruders started running near the white satellite antennas as background.

At that moment, in a trashcan, exploded the electronic artefact the red-haired teenager had left there. All the security personnel of that complex started attending to the outside bomb.

Lilith and her two guards ran on a field full of pretty flowers of many colours: lilac, orange, beige, and cyan. There were sprinklers to irrigate the grass. Those devices had visors, which pointed everywhere and emitted an imperceptible beep when noted a movement. Once those sensors noticed the intruders, the sprinklers changed their normal camera mode to thermal mode. They sent an alert and the security system started running automatically. The sprinklers stopped irrigating water on the field. Suddenly, emerged from the soil a system of weapons compounded by white crosses.

The bullets that left those weapons reached Lilith's colleagues. Their transparent dresses were damaged. In fact, the invisibility effect started vanishing from those dresses.

The green blood of the injured intruders stained the wonderful lilac and beige magnolias of that delightful garden. However, the rebels were making jumps in an incredible way to dodge the bullets. One of those fugitives fell on the field. The young white man laid dead on the soil, both Lilith and her other companion just left him behind. They continued their way jumping, but the bursts reached Lilith's second companion as well. She just saw her other friend die.

"Do it for our people," Lilith said to herself.

Some tears were leaving from Lilith's eyes, whilst continuing jumping to arrive at the principal hangar. There, all soldiers appeared at that BESA complex.

"Here Black Owl, we are under attack," one soldier warned by radio to all BESA Headquarters of the other Black Earth regions.

Lilith had on her right hand a device. She pressed on it a red button with her right thumb finger. Suddenly, some explosions occurred. They were produced by the bombs in the drainage and the bodies of her dead friends. The soldiers were stunned by those detonations. Then, a building of that complex and some runways used for fighter launches started imploding. Lilith was in front of the main hangar door, which was closed.

The soldiers stood round that intruder. They started shooting at her, but she made a spectacular counterclockwise jump. Her dress was almost destroyed, but she still had her face covered. Therefore, the soldiers could not see her precious face. Lilith gave a super jump and broke a window that was in the topmost part of that door to enter the hangar. On the other side, she fell so slowly into the hangar. Her hair levitated and the universe seemed to stop. Lilith started running, whilst the big silver metal door exploded behind her. She gave a jump to get in a silver fighter that was there.

The soldiers entered, shooting everywhere. Lilith already was in the fighter turning it on. She used the combat plane gun to shoot the soldiers. The militaries could not repel her attack. That fighter left the hangar ascending in a vertical way, breaking the roof. Military cars were arriving outside of the hangar, nonetheless Lilith had escaped.

On the combat plane, she was listening to a rock song related to revolution on her music device. Her fighter was so high, out of the soldier's guns. However, two fighters crossed the sky pursuing her.

Lilith put a target on those aircrafts. She could see them through the transparent cabin of her combat plane. The sun reflection crossed from the left towards the right side on Lilith's pilot helmet. Soon, six other fighters were arriving. They were aligned like a V-form. Lilith put her fighter in a vertical position pointing it towards the sun. She raised her combat plane so fast, where the pilots of the other fighters could not see her. Lilith reached high altitude until starting to freeze her aircraft. Then, her plane gave a turn pointing its frontal part towards the ground. After it, Lilith's fighter descended in free fall. A few seconds later, her combat plane sensors started warming by the air friction. In that way, Lilith could trigger six missiles, which followed the fighters that were below. Those torpedoes furrowed the sky in a mix of concave and convex ways. They reached each target making them burn in flames.

Lilith knew that there were still two fighters more on air seeking her. Effectively, those two combat planes appeared near Be Alpha Men City. She triggered the frontal gun of her aircraft against them.

Lilith started pursuing one of those fighters behind it. The aircraft in front of her was making manoeuvres to elude Lilith's bullets. Those two fighters were flying fast and near the peaks of some mountains.

They gave a curve almost rubbing the slope of a mountain and Lilith's enemy aircraft crashed into that massive hill.

Lilith was looking for the second fighter in pursuit. She elevated her fighter in a vertical way and gave a loop to place it behind her adversary. Lilith triggered all her armoury against other fighter, which exploded in fragments. That attack left an effluvium of fire on the firmament.

Meanwhile in the Fleuretty Region, Starlight's train was near the aquamarine colour lakes zone. The congress chairperson was on that transportation asleep on his leather dark-green sofa. He had a microbiology book on his legs. He was dressed in a beige imperial jacket with golden flowers embroidered over his lapel and cuffs. At his right side, there was a window with a beige colour curtain and a lamp made of gold at each side of the window frame. Outside the train, an immense cloud covered an enormous suspension bridge. That structure connected two hills separated by a big turquoise lake. At each side of the bridge, there were two large towers made of batholiths. The railway track was held by means of blue steel cables.

High up in the sky, a black point was moving towards the bridge. That strange phenomenon was becoming a big dark stain. Then, it converted into an enormous black gargoyle. That monster had wings like a dragon, with one curved nail-hook as a little foot to support each one of its wings at any surface. Its face was like a reptile. It had arms and legs like a man, but its hands and feet had claws. It had a long tail with picks as a lizard. The gargoyle was flying, arching its body to impulse itself, whilst it was screeching. Starlight left his oneiric universe and opened his eyes.

Another bad dream, he thought.

At that moment, some train service people started screaming. Aeda, Nemea, Meletea, Mr Aroth and the guards went towards Starlight's coach.

"My Lord, quick out of the window!" Mr Aroth said.

"Everybody get on the floor," one minder said.

The gargoyle was flying so fast approaching the bridge. That creature opened its big wings and crashed into that structure creating a sinusoidal wave perpendicular towards the railway track. The impact made an effect as if gravity did not exist on the train.

People and things were suspended making slow rotations. There were floating pieces of food, opened books, and laptops. Starlight and his friends were hugging at each one. Some guards were protecting them, whilst the waiters were avoiding the crockeries falling to the floor. Other minders were shooting at the beast with their guns.

One of those bullets went through one of the train windows. That shot continued its trajectory passing near a blue steel cord of the bridge, whilst the other cables were busting. The bullet entered the left eye of the creature.

At that moment, the gargoyle emitted a horrible screech and pushed back. It had its wings opened and wagging its long tail sharply. The cables were released from the bridge one by one, and the railway track started breaking. Again, the gargoyle hit the bridge, then the locomotive exploded.

The fire reached the rest of train coaches that were hanging. The creature made a loud scream, whilst its right green eye converted into Starlight's right eye. Then, the young politician woke up with a scared expression on his face.

"I had a false awakening."

Aeda, Nemea, and Meletea were with him in his room at the coach. Starlight was laid on a white bed with white pillows. He had on his forehead much perspiration. The girls were seeing him, whilst he got up. The girls had on imperial coats and semitransparent short dresses embroidered with wonderful flowers. They had princess golden shoes made by hand. Starlight was dressed in a beige royal jacket and a black trouser.

There was a luxurious dark wooden table at the right side of Starlight's bed. The table was decorated with embossing forms of swans and flowers. The train was leaving from the Fleuretty Region to arrive at the Kheter Region.

Suddenly, some minders entered Starlight's room. One of them was General Stealth.

"My Lord, ladies, it is appropriate to move towards the security coach."

"My friend. Is it something wrong?" Starlight asked him.

"Nothing my Lord, it is just for prevention," the general answered.

Near the train appeared in the sky a silver-grey fighter. That combat plane was leaving a Mach stele, which had the shape of an angel. The sunshine traversed the firmament making the fighter bright, whilst the train passed on a stone-bridge over a lake. The minders on the train were prepared to shoot at the fighter, with heavy weapons.

Starlight, and his friends, even Mr Aroth, were allocated in the security coach. In that part of the train, there were some special scuba diving dresses.

"Anti-radiation dresses," Meletea said.

She was amazed gazing at those yellow polymer clothes.

"General tell us the truth, please," Starlight requested.

"My Lord, a fighter was stolen from the BESA Headquarters in the Molog Region. It is approaching here. We were notified about it from Beta Persei Complex. In fact, that base was attacked a few minutes ago," General Stealth answered him.

"Why was I uninformed about that?"

"I am so sorry, my Lord."

"What must we do?" Starlight said to him.

"Please, put on the anti-radioactive scuba dive dresses. This is in case of an attack with radioactive weapons. Our soldiers are ready to provide the necessary protection to each one of you."

Lilith's fighter was approaching there. At that moment, she started shooting at the train with the big submachine gun of her fighter. The gun bursts impacted the rock supports of the bridge. Then, Lilith launched the last two torpedoes that were in the combat plane pylon. The two missiles crossed over the turquoise lake surface. A few seconds later, they impacted the supports of the bridge and generated thousands of rock pieces left through the air.

The locomotive and the last coach of the train exploded as well. The other coaches were trapped on the railway track. Lilith noted did not have more ammunitions and thought to crash her fighter into the train. Some minders continued shooting at the fighter. Another group of guards from a train window started to shoot at Lilith's aircraft with a fifty-calibre weapon. At that moment, General Stealth opened a little compartment of the coach where Starlight and his friends were. The four youngsters, Mr Aroth, and four armed minders jumped from the security coach to avoid the collision.

The two choppers of Starlight's guard appeared in the sky. They shot at Lilith's fighter with guns and torpedoes. Lilith opened her aquamarine eyes so wide.

"*As upme*," she just could say that.

The missiles from the helicopters impacted that combat plane. The sky had orange and red overtones made by the fire of Lilith's fighter explosion. After that, there were some train coaches in flames floating on the lake surface and others hanging from the bridge.

Starlight, his friends, and the minders were diving. The lake's surface reflected the fire explosion. At that point, three BESA attack helicopters appeared there to re-enforce the security of that area.

Starlight, and his team continued diving towards the lake shore. The brightness of a decreasing sun furrowed a red sky. Starlight and his group arrived at the shore. All of them were in excellent condition after that attack. Minutes later, General Stealth arrived there as well.

"Please my friend, find all photos and videos registered by the BESA security cameras. Please, you help my wounded minders and soldiers," Starlight said to Mr Stealth.

"Yes, my Lord."

At that moment, some soldiers and doctors descended from an attack helicopter, which was arriving there. They ran to Starlight and his group.

"Help to all the injured!" General Stealth ordered a soldier who was in the incoming group.

That black soldier ran and gave that order to one group of militaries, which was approaching there by boat. Another soldier gave a slim hologram plate to General Stealth.

"Sir, here is the report from the Molog Region, sir."

"Thank you, son," General Stealth said.

"Sir, permission to talk, sir."

"Of course," General Stealth said to him.

"Sir, all this material was given to us by my Captain Thunder. Today in the BESA Headquarters' attack in the Molog Region a person put a bomb in one garbage can. Moreover, there were three other terrorists in that military base. One of them took the fighter. That terrorist used a sophisticated propulsion device. She got elevated towards one small window on the upper part of a gate in one hangar. Our soldiers could not identify her. She had a special dress, which covered her face. You can watch that situation on the hologram plate, sir."

Starlight took the word watching the hologram screen. "That must be a wave device because I see no combustion. Evermore, those attacks were in public. They want to have a show. They want to be recognised, but not discovered."

General Stealth put his right hand over the soldier's left shoulder.

"Thanks son. Go wait for instructions."

"Sir, yes sir," the brunette soldier answered.

Then, that soldier gave thirteen steps away.

CHAPTER SIX

The Evil Actions

The general walked away a few steps alone to read the hologram report with Starlight.

"My Lord, these are the videos captured by the street cameras each day that you were under an attack. Please look at here; the terrorist was on a black superbike in Tartarusm Square's attack. She used a wave disturbing device on her dress. For that reason, she could blur her own image on camera. Here, we can watch the accomplices. I think they had the same device." General Stealth pointed at the hologram screen.

"Have we got their DNA?"

"No, my Lord. We have not done it yet. We do not know who they are really. In fact, if the terrorist's body is here on the water, my soldiers can find it."

The general turned and gave an order out loud. "Soldiers, I need a complete revision of all this area. I need the body of the terrorist now! Check to the last fragment rock of this area. Come on soldiers, hasten! We have not got all day!"

A group of soldiers started running to execute General Stealth's order.

Starlight continued talking with the General, "I think they are a network, but who could be their leader? I need a deep investigation of all my people and their movements. In fact, you bring secret agents. General, I need copies of all the security cameras of the cities where the terrorists had been. It is so important."

"Yes, my Lord."

At that moment, many people were approaching there to see Starlight.

"I need all these people outside of my security perimeter!" General Stealth shouted.

"Guys, please try finding an anti-terrorist screen and a bulletproof jacket. I am going to give a speech," Starlight said to his security staff.

"My Lord, it is unthinkable. If more terrorists are still around here, they will try attacking you again," the general said to Starlight.

"It is better. If they are here, they could listen to the things that I am going to say," Starlight said.

"So be it, my Lord." The general made a bow.

Then, some minders ran to find Starlight's requirements, whilst others helped the wounded.

Mr Aroth, Aeda, Meletea, and Nemea ran worried to Starlight.

"My Lord, are you going to give a speech now? It is risky for you," Aeda said to him.

"Lady Aeda and friends, I must do it and I am going to do it now."

General Stealth gave the permission that one journalist borrowed her microphone and camera for Starlight's discourse. Minders and soldiers assembled so fast a kind of atrium for that purpose. Many people from the Fleuretty and Kether Region started meeting there. It was because that bridge represented the frontier between those two regions.

There, people started cheering the young congressman, "Starlight, Starlight, Starlight."

The minders approached covering Starlight with a new bulletproof royal jacket. That coat had green colour and was decorated with swans, and snakes embroidered with golden threads. Starlight was at the atrium and started giving his speech, whilst Mr Aroth was holding the microphone.

"My people. Today, a terrorist attack occurred. It was not against me, it was against all our people. All the regions, Black Earth, Pandemonical Continent, and Sattrin Earth are more important than all. Today, I am here facing the terrorists and saying to them in the name of my people that we are unafraid. For that reason, I am going to continue my travel by train."

At that moment, people were amazed. Starlight continued, "To take a plane at this moment, is equal to say, terrorists, you won. They could not strew terror on our sacred soil. We are going to be standing to face them. Under the guide of gods, I am going to defend all my people and my land from any kind of violence, or terrorism. I say to the victims of this attack that I am with them. I am going to give them all my support and my attention. Thank you."

People, journalists, soldiers, and security corps were applauding him. Meletea, Nemea, and Aeda had tears in their eyes, whilst they applauded him as well. At that moment, from the Kether Region appeared another luxurious silver train.

The new train had an aquamarine central line instead of red. Over that stripe was a strange name; Ezlalba. Each train had its own name in ancient language. Starlight, his friends, and team started boarding that train.

Starlight took a big rest. A few hours later, he got up from his black leather chair and saw his friends. They were working in helping the victims and families of the attack. Starlight joined them checking the hologram laptops and calling all government entities.

That train coach seemed like a stock exchange market. There, people were running, calling by phone, and taking notes in hologram agendas. Aeda was calling to the Minister for Defence and Nemea to the chairperson of the Kether National Hospital at Hur-Appean Reich City. She made a call for the chairperson of L'hôpital Rue des Roses in New-Light City as well.

Meanwhile, Starlight's train continued its path; something important was happening in Befomet City.

In a luxurious club of that city, arrived three black limousines. Three valet parking received them. From those cars, descended three men: Messrs Paulge, Thade, and Raw. In that club, there was at the entrance a water fountain with an angel sculpture made of marble. It had its wings opened and its right arm extended trying to touch the sky. The three senators ascended the porch stairs to enter that club and their security personnel as well.

The principal double door had white colour and black rectangular glass panels. In fact, that place was the Lexabyssi Congress Club. Those senators were walking near a pool where there were other senators and some models. Messrs Paulge, Thade, and Raw entered a private room.

In that place, there were many waitresses, a big table with crabs, and white wine. The three senators sat down on wide dark leather chairs and started smoking tropical tobaccos and drinking some whisky. They held their canes of dark wood by their right hands. Suddenly, the three senators made a signal, and those waitresses left the room. They left them alone, and then the three politicians started talking.

"What about the situation given the recent acts?" Senator Paulge asked.

"Well, all things had happened according to the celestial plan. What is your opinion, Senator Thade?" Senator Raw asked.

"Yes, the path of events has pointed to the principal objective. We are going to be widely recompensed for it, Cheers!"

"Cheers Senator Paulge!" the other two senators said.

Then, they raised their cups.

Meanwhile, in the Kether Region, the night had fallen. Starlight was writing on his computer and establishing some callings. He continued to worry about wounded people and their families. Then, he watched the clock and saw it marked the three hours in the morning.

He gazed at the horizon through his train window. He looked at the dark sky full of stars and noticed a kind of shadow of a gargoyle. Starlight thought it was an enemy fighter, but it was a shadow formed by the clouds.

"I need to take a rest," he told himself.

He got up from his chair, turned off his hologram computer, and walked through a luxurious corridor of his train coach. That hall had walls decorated with paintings of small figures of jockeys riding their horses. There was a dark red carpet on the floor and little tables, whose supports had an arched shape. Plates full of butter cookies were on those tables. Starlight entered each room of his friends, starting with Aeda, Meletea, and Nemea. He sheltered them one by one with their blankets. He gave them a kiss on their forehead. Then, he arrived at Mr Aroth's room; Starlight merely opened (not entirely), the door and saw him asleep.

"Thank you, my friend," he said to Mr Aroth quietly.

The night brought the rain, which fell in a diagonal way. Those drops seemed like pieces of paper floating on air by the reflecting of locomotive frontal light. Starlight went towards his room and sat down on his bed.

"What a long day, good night, Mr Starlight. Tomorrow will be a better day," he said to himself.

The next day, the light from the sun touched some little hills. On the topmost part of one of them, there was a white castle. It was the New Swan Rock Castle, which in Ketherean Language meant Neu-Schwan-Stein.

Starlight's train crossed near there and the girls took many photos of that fortress from their rooms. They were enjoying the landscapes and that little moment of peace. They did not know the evil actions the universe had prepared for them.

Starlight's train continued its path and days later it arrived at a small village, at north of Sanct-Real City in the Habraxas Region. That place had a precious sea of seven colours. The houses in that region were small and their walls had many tones. Those houses were embedded on the cliffs near the shore.

Once there, Starlight and his friends descended from the train to take a rest of that trip. They arrived at a small public beach resort. They stayed there a few hours before continuing their path. The site was nice and uncrowded. Starlight and his friends did put off their coats and jackets. The girls seized that situation to clothe with their tropical A-line style dresses. Those dresses had green, black, and blue colours, and each one had different prints compounded by flowers. The three pretty girls had hats of beige colours. Each hat had a stripe of orange, violet, and purple tones.

Starlight had on a white waistcoat made of silky fabric embroidered with trees of soft blue colour with a white trouser, fitted at his ankles. Luxurious white beach shoes covered his feet. That footwear had embroidered trees with the same colour as his waistcoat. Starlight was sitting on the beach staring at the magnificence of the sea. Meletea approached him.

"Why are you so disconnected, my Lord?"

"Lady Meletea, I feel so bad and uncomfortable. I am thinking about all the people that were left wounded in those attacks against me. It is so unfair for them. They are my people and must not suffer by my politics career."

"My Lord, you passed all these nights working for each one of them. You were brave and strong enough to give your speech after that attack. You can say to the entire world that neither terrorists nor assassins are going to break the courage of our people."

"Yes, but…"

"My Lord, I have a question for you. What will happen on the day that you are walking through the shadows? I want to know if those people will come helping you," she replied smiling.

At that moment, both were looking at the beach. Sunshine was reflecting on the sea producing thousands of little lights on the tide waves. Then, Nemea and Aeda arrived.

Meletea got up.

"My Lord, you should think about it," she said to him, then she went from there.

Starlight continued looking at the sea. A few minutes later, the three girls appeared there again. They were dressed in two-piece swimsuits to enjoy the sun. Quickly, many men were seeing them admiring their beauty.

At the end of that day, Starlight and his friends boarded the train after their rest. They would continue their travel towards the Ahvitchi Region. Meanwhile, the train left the Habraxas Region some people waved with immense joy many flags of red, green, and white colours.

The frontier between the Habraxas and Ahvitchi Region was compounded by a natural mountain system called Ahvitchi Rock Wall. In that location, the weather was so different from the public beach resort. A cold fog invaded the landscape, and the trees lost their green vestment by a mixture of white and grey colour. Heaven was full of brightening stars illuminating Ezlalba's trajectory. Those grey mountains were higher, and their picks were covered by the snow. The view of that landscape was opaque and lugubrious by the mist, which reigned in that place.

The train got near the entrance of a tunnel in the mountain. At that moment, the darkness fell together with the snow, whilst the train was traversing that tunnel. Suddenly, it could be heard on air as choral voices singing. *"Ny up, seed Morfim fee as not as. Ny up, seed Morfim fee as not as."*

The tunnel had an ascending slope. One hour and a half later, the train reached the other side. Once the train left the tunnel, it could see a white soil and a dark-grey sky. Some birds were flying between the cypresses through the fog. The railway track was almost invisible, except by security red lines of light at each side. The sky started projecting some lights of different forms and colours as green, soft blue, and purple. The effect of those lights on heaven was a wonderful scene. Starlight was seeing them through his room window. That aurora borealis robbed a smile from the young congressman, whilst the night started accompanying his journey.

Although the train had an excellent heating system, people on the Ezlalba wore jackets and coats.

A new day had come, and the weather was a little friendlier. The fog was vanishing, and the sun appeared quite more. The train continued its path and the fjords started appearing in the landscape. The sea shocked against cliffs as if water would want to break the continental shore. The sea had a wonderful indigo colour singing for the shore a deep blue melody. Minutes later, some houses could be seen at both sides of the railway track. Their walls were made in wood with hanging flowers, and their roofs were painted with blood-red colour. In front of their principal doors, some rods held flags of the Ahvitchi Region. Those flags were of cyan and yellow colours.

The Ezlalba was passing in front of those small towns, whilst people were holding and waving their flags. It was because those Hur-Appeans were so happy with Starlight's arrival.

Few hours later, Starlight and his friends arrived at Blue-Ice City. The congress chairperson was in his train room reading a book. At that moment, a guard knocked on his door.

"My Lord, it is time."

"Thank you," Starlight said to him.

Blue-Ice City had architecture well preserved, old buildings of three until six decks. They had big roofs like belfries with conical triangles shapes. In that city, the buildings were grouped along the Lerage River. Over it, there were many bridges decorated with red and orange flowers at its lateral balustrades. In the same way, those bridges had bronze General Be Alpha Men statues. They were dressed in winter jackets. The centre of Blue-Ice City was full of people. Most of those citizens had white faces and blond or red hair. Their eyes were grey, green, or blue. Some of them were climbing a General Be Alpha Men statue to see the train. Others started leaving from their houses waving the Ahvitchi Region and Black Earth flags as well. They were clamming, "Starlight, Starlight, Starlight."

The Ezlalba stopped on the platform numbered twenty-three. A great security scheme was established in that place. Guards created a corridor for Starlight and his friends.

They descended from the train and walked on a red carpet of that corridor. Three black limousines were outside of that train station waiting for them. The building of that train station had two parts. The first had horizontal elongated domes of crystal on the roof, where the trains left or entered the platforms. The second one was the administrative part. Its frontal part had walls with green leaves hanging from them. There was a higher turquoise belfry with a white clock as a roof. On its spire was an Ahvitchi Region flag.

Starlight just stopped his walk and said to Blue-Ice City people, "My friends. I am going to defend our land until the end. It is my duty for you and my master Malmo who borne in this land. Thank you."

People went crazy for glee, whilst a blonde kid with grey eyes approached there. The kid wanted to give Starlight a flower crown. The first reaction of Starlight's guards was getting the child apart. However, the congress president smiled at the kid and received the crown from that child's hands.

Starlight put the crown on his head and continued his way towards the black limousine followed by his security guards. He gave thanks to those people making the ancient greeting. Starlight made it in remembrance to preserve all the things in heaven and earth.

The congress chairperson's committee boarded the three limousines. Six black armoured sports utility vehicles secured them. Three of those vehicles were in front of the limousines and three behind. The caravan continued with six police motorcycles. The last part of that security scheme was composed of three military attack helicopters in the air.

One of the primary highways in Blue-Ice City connected the train station and a location near the governor's castle outside the city. One of the lanes of that highway was closed by Starlight's caravan.

People continued waving Black Earth flags, whilst Starlight's convoy passed through the highway. Three quarters of hours later, the congress caravan was so near the hill where the governor's castle was. The limousines and police motorcycles of the caravan got an ascending thoroughfare, which ended in the governor's fortress. That road was decorated with torches and royal knights from the Ahvitchi Region were guarding that way. They were in a stand-up position at both sides of the way like statues. Those knights were dressed in wide uniforms made by stripes with colours from that region. They had silver helmets, boots with embossed swans, and bronze lances in the shape of a trident.

The afternoon was falling on Blue-Ice City. The sun's orange rays reflected on the grey castle walls, and its towers as well. The governor's bastion was established on the top of that hill on a small lake with a shape of lotus flower. From that castle, it was possible to see the magnificent ocean and fjords. That castle was one of the first constructions established on Black Earth.

CHAPTER SEVEN

A Day in Life of Eternity

Lilith was born in that castle as an only child; her father was Ahvitchi Region's governor. On one dark and rainy night, Lilith's parents left a political meeting. They took their diplomatic limousine and sat in the backseats of that car with Lilith. She was a baby; her mother was carrying her. According to witnesses, a ray fell from the sky, and the driver lost control of the limousine. The big car rolled down an abyss near the fjords. Then, the diplomatic car exploded. A few hours later, police officers and guards arrived there finding the car burned. Only Lilith survived the accident. She was near the limousine. A velvet red mantle embroidered with golden threads was sheltering her. The figure on the mantle represented a feminine form with wings, accompanied by two lions, one snake, and two owls at its sides. Those symbols represented the prosperity and wisdom under the Ahvitchi Region traditions. The reflection of the brilliant moon fell on the baby's aquamarine eyes that night. She had a pretty smile on her face.

CHAPTER EIGHT

The Colour and the Shape

People from the Ahvitchi Region loved the governor and his wife so much. They were Lilith's adoptive parents. Originally, they were her butlers. After the accident Mrs and Mr Dushe decided to adopt her. Their love for Lilith made them obtain the entire regions respect. They signed the issues for the adoption and refused the lands, titles, and monetary wealth from the royal lineage. Mrs and Mr Dushe were elegant and well educated. Those characteristics made them adequate to be the little girl's tutors.

Starlight remembered Lilith's life history because he had read it previously. He and his friends descended from the three black limousines. The governor and his wife received them with a special diplomatic protocol. Starlight and his team presented them their corresponding diplomatic greetings. They put their right hands over their own chests making the ancient greeting.

Starlight and his friends were so tired by all the events that happened, and they wanted to take a big rest. The governor understood that situation widely. For that reason, he offered Starlight and his court a private dinner and the best guest castle suites.

The time for the banquet had arrived, and the night was covered with its dark mantle. There was a sculpture made of gold hanging on a wall in the principal dining room of the castle. It was formed by a big circle with many alligators joined between them. Starlight gazed at that wall surprised.

"Yes, my Lord. The sketch of that artwork was drawn by our little girl," The governor said to him, referring to Lilith. "She was seven-years-old when she drew that piece of art."

"It is quite interesting. A gifted girl," the congress chairperson said.

Then, the governor got up from the table to offer a toast. Mr Dushe extended his right arm and hand holding his cup pointing towards a window.

"For our lord, Starlight."

Outside the castle, the black sky was decorated with stars as brushstrokes on a painting. Suddenly, two light bursts with different colours traversed diagonally that dark image, and then they exploded forming two balls of fireworks, which illuminated the sky. Many light circles exploded in the heavens. First, several small lights appeared and then the big ones. Then, they formed a pyramid repeating it several times until creating the Black Earth flag.

Starlight and his friends toasted with their wine cups as well.

Then, the youthful congress president asked, "Why is not Lilith with us?"

"My Lord, my little girl is in Befomet City finishing some academic things at Royal Imperium University. She is going to take her private jet to be here tomorrow, my Lord," Mrs Dushe answered him.

"Thank you for everything. Mrs and Mr Dushe, I am so grateful for this," Starlight said to them.

Mrs Dushe took the right hand of her husband and looked at his eyes. Then she turned her head to see Starlight.

"It is our duty, my Lord," she said to him, smiling.

Near the castle, the fireworks continued producing swans and big green snakes moving in the air. Those sparkles were disappearing through the night because a new day was caressing the sky again.

Hours later, two fighters with the shape of bats furrowed Blue-Ice City firmament. Then, passed Lilith's private jet escorted by two other fighters. She and her guards were arriving at the military base of BESA in Ahvitchi Region.

Lilith wore a precious semitransparent dress embroidered with red roses. She had on a large black coat decorated with golden roses. On her head, Lilith wore an ornament like an aureole decorated with several jewels.

Moments later once in the fortress, she went to see Starlight who was in one of the gardens. Lilith took a small boat to traverse a lake to meet with him. The little ship's edges had small swan heads painted with golden colour. In its frontal part there was a big swan head as well. The boat hull was decorated with turquoise colour and some dark blue jewels.

"*Temo febirt son hied, hinga mieden him on hni,*" Lilith said.

Starlight was walking in a field of sunflowers next to the lake. On its surface, were floating many white lotus flowers. Heaven had a fire colour by the dawning sun.

Lilith descended from the boat, whilst Starlight held her right hand. Then, she gave him a little courtesy.

"I appreciate that you have not declined my invitation. My heart is so happy to see you again."

Starlight looked at her.

"Why before I met you in university, I saw you like a shadow hidden behind the water curtains?"

"The answer is easy, my Lord. You were always the smart guy in high school and university. Sometimes I thought you would never want to be my friend. A boy like you spends your time always with models or actresses, and not with one geek girl like me."

Starlight changed his facial expression.

"When I was studying at Beliar High School, I was a poor genius boy in one uptown school. You had been the girl with the crown, so your comment had not sense, my lady."

"Yes. I know it, but you are older than me. I had always been two courses behind you. I was ashamed to start a conversation with you. I just thought about talking with you about… you and I are adopted. It identified me a lot with you."

Starlight looked at her tenderly.

"We just have an age difference of two years. You could talk with me, whenever you wanted. However, I have another question, my lady. Why do I see you in my dreams?"

"Because… I recognised you on my mind as well."

Both took their hands and walked through the sunflowers field, whilst a group of small and thin green lizards were walking on the lake. The young couple talked more and then arrived at the castle. Minutes later, the main square of that fortress was full of journalists and politicians of Black Earth.

Half an hour later, Starlight was walking on a red carpet in that place. He was dressed in white boots embroidered with swans of golden colour, a white trouser, and a turquoise jacket embroidered with golden swans as well. Starlight and his friends walked on that red carpet and then they ascended by a scaffold decorated with white roses and violet Mandragora Autumnalis. They sat down on white wood chairs located behind a big table. Mr and Mrs Dushe and Lilith were there as well. At that moment, a flock of Hur-Appean Ampelis birds furrowed the sky.

In the square, was the Marching Band of the Ahvitchi Region. Its musicians had trumpets, drums, and clarinets. They were invoked to ancient gods with the precious music notes emerging from their instruments. That was a familiar sound for Starlight. The Ahvitchi Region childrens chorus pronounced with their clear voices a verse: *"Temo febirt son hied, hinga mieden him on hni."*

Outside the castle, people were celebrating with much glee. They had many small pom poms for feasts, and the sky was adorned with multicoloured pieces of paper.

People were clapping, "Starlight, Starlight, Starlight."

Mr Dushe got up from his chair. The band ended its playing, and everybody stopped her or his chats or claps.

The governor started speaking.

"Fellows. Today is a grandeur day for our lives. We have in our presence the hope to have the best future. A young man that is going to change the face of the universe. Here is our Congress President, Mr Starlight."

People exclaimed again in unison with glee, "Starlight, Starlight, Starlight!"

The young politician got up.

"Thank you, my friends. Let me express, nothing is impossible for our people. We can do anything in the name of peace in our land." Then, he exclaimed. "Yes, we can!"

"Yes, we can. Yes, we can. Yes, we can!" there, all the people exclaimed as well.

Starlight was smiling and then tried joining his hands palms to emphasise his speech. At that moment, people in the square were seeing Starlight taking the sun in his hands. That was an optical effect by the sun's position on the sky behind him.

Starlight continued, "We must follow the light of education, understanding and peace. We must be as General Be Alpha Men, the light bearer! Our minds and hearts will guide us for a better future. A future traced by our people, by all of yours. gods blessed my people. Thank you."

At that moment, a military helicopter shadow was over Starlight's head. He looked at that war machine. The chopper shadow covered the right part of his face. It was not the only one helicopter there. Three other military choppers with soldiers were rounding the castle to give more security for Starlight, governors, and all the guests. Police and military corps compounded a big security ring to avoid people entering the castle.

Hours later, Starlight went to take a rest. In the topmost part of a tower of that castle, there was a luxury room for Starlight. That room had a black piano, a few white leather sofas, a big chimney made of grey marble, and a dark wooden shelf for books. The walls had a soft brown colour, and the edges of the windows had a white wood frame. Near the main door of that room, there was a painting of a goat head. In addition, there were few vases filled with white roses and violet Mandragora Autumnali as well.

At that moment, Starlight was with General Stealth in that room.

"My Lord, my team and I revised all evidence from the attacks and believed that the terrorist had free access to a disturbed wave device. It could make her seem like a ghost. However, the only one person in the world that is developing such technology is you. Moreover, we could not find the fighter pilot's body on the lake. In fact, we do not know if the terrorist is deceiving us by making us believe that he is a girl."

"Amazing, a disturbance wave model combined with my special polymer dress is unbelievable. General, I need a complete report of all people that had recently visited my office. I thought that we can investigate the visitors of Beliar High School, and Royal Imperium University laboratories as well. Moreover, I am going to require a judicial order to track all mobile phones from laboratory personnel of those institutions," Starlight said to the general.

"The former is easy, but the latter is risky. It is related to personal interception themes." The general emphasized.

"I know it, but if my developments fell into the wrong hands... It will be the greatest disaster." Starlight interrupted him.

At that moment, a knock sounded on the room door. A few seconds later, the gate opened slowly. The person who was entering the room was Lilith.

"Oh, I am sorry, my Lord. I did not know you had a rendezvous."

"My lady, there is no problem," Starlight and the general answered her.

Starlight was still clothed with the same vestments in his speech. However, Lilith had changed her attire to an elegant sleeveless miniskirt dress which was fixed to her precious figure. She had on black suede boots embroidered with golden flowers, and was wearing a small crown full of diamonds on her head.

Lilith gave a few steps into that room.

"General. May I show the fjords to, my Lord Starlight tomorrow?"

He drew a friendly smile on his face.

"My lady, I am just a server of, my Lord."

"For me, it is a great honour to visit the fjords with you," Starlight said to Lilith.

"I am at your service, my Lord. My lady. I must be absent," the general said.

Starlight gave him a fraternal hug.

"My friend, please help me with that theme. I will be in contact with you later."

"So, my Lord. I will see you tomorrow at morning," Lilith said to Starlight, making a courtesy and to the military as well.

Both General Stealth and the girl left Starlight's room. The congress chairperson was seeing his suite door closing.

It will be better to think about another theme. Starlight thought.

The next day, two bicycles left from the castle, one black and another white. The former rode by Starlight and the latter by Lilith. Those two bikes went so fast on a hill, which had a splendorous view of Blue-Ice City. Soon, they reached an ancient stone way. Pines branches were at both sides of the path caressing the faces and hairs of those young. They were enjoying the ride as two little children, whilst the orange, blue heaven was showing its face over them. Suddenly, a big military attack helicopter appeared in the air that was following them for their security.

"Are we far yet?" Starlight asked her, whilst he was looking at the descending way.

"My Lord, you must go fast," Lilith answered him with grace.

"So, reach me if you can," Starlight said to her, smiling.

Starlight rode rapidly until Lilith could not see him.

"Wow, he is really faster than me," she said to herself.

They arrived at a zone with beautiful fjords, the Abysm Gate. There, the sea hit with strength the fjords. The tide was melting by magma, which came from the Abysm Volcano. Nearby, there was a lighthouse on an isolated island. At the topmost part of that construction was an inscription:

Beati luce.

There, ocean water had a dark blue colour produced by tidal force, which liquefied the seafloor algae. From the highest hill part, it could see the volcano peak covered by snow. The lowest part of the fjords had dark limestone rocky foundations. It was a precious phenomenon from nature keyed by the geological ages.

Starlight was seeing the green in Lilith's eyes.

"Thank you, my lady for this ride. I am so happy to be in the Abysm Gate with you."

Lilith gazed at him with her bright green eyes.

"My Lord, for me it is a great honour to bring you towards the Abysm Gate. I want you to feel at home."

Starlight held her hands.

"So, thank you for taking me home again."

In the bottom part of the fjords was a crow flock standing on the limestones. Then those birds left flying.

"I will walk happily on the crow's path near the abyss, holding your white hand. The laugh is in my soul, where the beast is hiding. In the end of creation, you would be on my mind," Starlight said to her.

"It is the prettiest verse that I had ever listened to, my Lord," she answered him.

"Well, my lady. I crossed the universe to say it."

Starlight and Lilith continued talking, whilst their two bicycles were laid on the soil. The silhouette of a military attack helicopter was still over them. The couple admired the view a few moments more. Then, they started riding their bicycles again with a spectacular rainbow as background.

Hours later, the orange-red heaven denoted the first stars of the night, which were appearing on the celestial vault with a waning moon.

Once in the castle again, Starlight went towards a private reunion with some governors from other regions. That meeting was in one magnificent room of the fortress. There were small flags of the Ahvitchi Region and Black Earth hanging on the walls. Starlight would sign some government issues that congress commissioned for him. It was for the implementation of new military tests, which he would lead.

After that reunion, Starlight gave thanks to the governors and then offered greetings to some journalists that were there as well. General Stealth was there, and then he approached Starlight.

"Just in time, as a good Netflimtian," Starlight said to him.

The general smiled and said to him in a low voice, "My Lord, I obtained all the reports of each person in the science laboratories of Beliar High School and Royal Imperium University. My Lord, I did not find anything bizarre or abnormal. There is nothing strange recorded by cameras related to personal access in your congress office. About the wave disturbance dress, we could not find anything, my Lord. The terrorist is like a ghost."

"My friend, the phantoms did not exist. They are a representation of the other entities. They are in another rank of perception."

"What do you want to do, my Lord?"

"Someone of my extreme confidence is related to all this. I need to get back towards Befomet City. I am going to be there in two days."

The general gazed at him.

"My Lord, I am going to do everything as possible to find the intruder."

"Well, so be it general. That wisdom will be with you, my friend."

Starlight gave a fraternal hug to General Stealth. Then, the congress chairperson left that meeting saying goodbye to everyone. He went towards his room. Alone on his bed, Starlight drank a red wine glass and ate one butter cookie. He walked towards his room window to see the firmament.

How wonderful is this night? I am enjoying its colour and its shape, he thought.

Through Starlight's window, it could see the lights of Blue-Ice City. Some commercial planes were flying towards the airport. Suddenly, one shooting star furrowed the sky. At that moment, someone knocked on Starlight's room door.

"Please enter," Starlight said.

There, the door opened, and the three beautiful girls appeared. Nemea, Meletea, and Aeda entered.

"Good night, my Lord," at the same time, the three girls said.

"My ladies, it is a great pleasure. Please take a seat, do you want to eat or drink something?"

They sat down and Nemea took the word.

"My Lord, are you sure about that enterprise? It is like a cat entering a black box."

Starlight took the slim and pretty hands of those three wonderful girls and looked at them gently.

"Friends, we must reach the peace and union of our people. It is necessary for the evolution of our society. Everything will be fine my ladies. I promise it."

"We trust in you, my Lord," Aeda said to him.

Then, she changed the conversation theme.

"Are you going to come with us to the party tomorrow?"

"Yes, I am going to be there."

The four young were sitting on the big leather sofa, then turned on a big hologram television device and started to watch a movie.

Meanwhile, Lilith was in the cryobiology laboratory of the Royal Imperium University again. In that dark place, she was walking among some crypts as she did before. Lilith was dressed in completely black colour. At that moment, a being with an eagle peak opened one of its eyes. Another being with white owl face was in another of those crypts.

Starlight woke up with sweat on his forehead. He glanced at a small digital clock; it was eleven thirty-four at night. He turned and observed the girls that were asleep on the sofa. The hologram screen still was on.

Another nightmare, Lilith was in the cryobiology lab.

Maybe, I am stressed by the attacks. Tomorrow is the party with my friends, and I must sleep, he thought.

CHAPTER NINE

The Empty of Vacuum

The stars of that night started moving so fast in a circular path. Simultaneously, the black sky colour became turquoise and finally cyan. The sun appeared illuminating the fjords and gave them a marvellous energy. The cypresses emitted a splendorous woody odour. On that new day, Starlight was running on a stone path. It was the same path connecting the fjords and the castle. Starlight was dressed in a long beige sleeve polo T-shirt and shorts. The T-shirt had the number twenty-three embroidered in red on the right arm and back. Suddenly, he stopped his workout. He wanted to see the fjords.

Really is so wonderful, he thought.

At that moment, Lilith appeared there. She was running as well. Lilith was dressed in a polo clothing style of soft turquoise colour, which had a yellow stripe from the frontal upper right towards the frontal left down part.

She looked at Starlight with tenderness.

"Good morning, my Lord. Are you going to go to the party tonight? I will do it in your honour."

He petted her blonde hair.

"Thank you, my lady. Of course, I am going to be there."

Then, they continued running and talking a lot.

The hours passed and the afternoon arrived. A dark red-orange sky caught the early fireworks, which left the castle. At the harbour of Blue-Ice City were arriving many luxury yachts coming from the thirteen regions of Black Earth. Great personalities, young politicians, artists, and entrepreneurs arrived there. Limousines were waiting for them to take the route from the harbour towards the castle.

A queue of limousines was ascending on the stone way of the castle's principal gate. There were many journalists and photographers, and a news channel chopper was in the sky near the fortress. That helicopter was broadcasting the event to all territories of Black Earth. Below, many journalists were interviewing each celebrity that arrived there.

Small yellow butterflies were in the air. There were some birds near the castle. One of those little birds was flying alone. At its right, there was the burgundy-coloured sky. At the other side, there was a slope of an olive-green hill. The bird trajectory had a semi-circular path, and its flapping was fast and then held. Finally, that Ampelis arrived at one window of the castle outside the party.

At the interior of the castle, people were amazed. They looked up towards the inner roof and could see a crystal dome. The night had fallen, and the lights of that dome described the sky chart. People could find many constellations there.

The music was coming from a big orchestra, which had a sensual black singer with a powerful voice. The security was strong both on the outside and inside of the castle. Guests into the fortress were enjoying a long table decorated with an excellent buffet. It was possible to find the world's best food.

Mr Aroth and Starlight were walking together into the castle. The congress chairperson was dressed in a short imperial jacket of lime colour embroidered with white roses. Its lapel and sleeves had embellished silver owls. He had on black trousers with black roses embroidered as a lateral stripe on each leg, and imperial golden boots as well. Mr Aroth had an imperial leather jacket and black trousers and boots. They were holding their cocktails in their left hands. Many people sought to see Starlight to talk with him, but he just desired to be with his friends. The three young girls Aeda, Nemea, and Meletea approached Starlight and Mr Aroth.

"Hey boys. Why are you so bored? Come on, join us at the party," the girls said.

Then, Meletea took the right hand of Mr Aroth. Nemea, and Aeda did the same with Starlight. The girls went with them towards the centre of the principal room to dance to the rhythm of the music. Outside the castle, the fireworks illuminated the night.

"My Lord, did you know it?" Meletea asked.

"Yes, Lady Meletea," Mr Aroth interrupted her. "The idea to go towards South Earth to get peace and become one nation."

"What do you think about it?"

"My lady. Really, I am worried about that. However, I am, and I will be with, my Lord in all his projects."

Meanwhile, Aeda and Nemea were dancing with Starlight. Nemea broke the ice.

"My Lord, you dance so well."

"My Lord, your feet are flying like clouds," Aeda said to him.

"My feet are as heavy as the armour of a humble warrior," Starlight said to them, smiling.

"My Lord, please be careful in your enterprise," Aeda said to him.

Starlight hugged them and smiled.

"My ladies, do not be worried. I am not going to be a fortune's toy."

The song ended, and Lilith descended slowly from the second floor by the stairs. Her blonde hair was gorgeous, and it had a little silver rhodium crown with small rose diamonds. Lilith wore a stunning red sleeveless dress, compounded by a veil fabric embroidered with small flowers. She had on a beautiful diamond ring and a tiny gold collar.

On the second floor, General Stealth was talking with Officer Flussman (who had arrived there that day). They were checking the event security. General Stealth gave an order to one soldier that was on the second floor as well. "Son, help the lady."

The muscular black soldier assisted Lilith down the stairs. That soldier was holding her right hand, whilst she continued descending so slowly. Everybody was amazed seeing her even Starlight. Lilith was in the centre of stairs as a vanish point in that passage. Two columns were at both sides of the stairs, and the dome was on them illuminating all with its constellations. The black and white rectangular tiles of the floor contrasted with those beige marble columns. On the first floor, Lilith turned to her aide.

"Thank you, sir."

He made her a bow.

"My lady."

Then Lilith gazed at everybody.

"Thanks for coming tonight to Starlight's party. Enjoy this soiree, my friends."

Then, streamers exploded launching thousands of big white rose petals through the air. Intelligence personnel and artificial security systems were heedful to every detail in the party as well. The older people were in another big room sitting, talking, and enjoying the orchestra, and the party relaxer than the young guests.

There was a stage in the main room, where the young guests were. At that moment, there appeared a rock band of three musicians. Green laser lights left the stage, which reflected on some crystal party balls. There, the young were dancing and making the ancient greeting with their hands. That room was full of people. Lilith was with Starlight talking so loudly.

"My Lord, this is a gift for you, listen to it please."

The empty of vacuum was filled with notes from an electric guitar. A big light from a reflector illuminated Starlight's face.

"This is for our notable guest," the singer said.

The band started playing a song with the name of Black Earth's congress chairperson. Starlight was so happy and the rest of the people in that room were singing that song. The music sounded so great.

Lilith held Starlight's hands, and everybody started jumping. A flying object passed over them projecting the crowd on a hologram screen. For the first time, Starlight felt like he was part of a real party. Outside the castle, the fireworks still exploded on that night. Minutes passed gracefully and everybody enjoyed that meeting.

Starlight left for a moment on a balcony. Lilith was behind him, and they were leaning on the ochre balustrades of the terrace. They were seeing the horizon, towards the south of the Pandemonical Continent. That enormous natural wall could be seen from any place on Black Earth. That barrier divided Black Earth and South Earth. The aspect of that wall was tenebrous. Black clouds and a big dark fog covered it. The darkness on that part of the planet came from the shadow of the asteroid belt around Sattrin Earth. Then, one thunder fell.

"My Lord, fears not the distant storm. Rays are beautiful things created for you my precious boy," Lilith said to him.

Then, she reached down and pulled a five-leafed clover from the small garden of the balcony. She gave that present to Starlight.

He gazed at her with tenderness and received the clover.

"My lady, we should return to the party. I want not to bore you with a speech now."

The couple entered the big room again.

A few hours later, people started leaving from the castle, when the celebration had ended. The sun had not appeared on firmament yet. The moon was still smiling, rounded by a dark sky. Starlight and his friends went to their respective suites in the castle to take a rest.

The next day, Starlight would prepare his luggage for the trip towards the Netflimt Region.

Once in the new day, a caravan of seven black sports utility vehicles was ready to take Starlight and his retinue towards the airport of Blue-Ice City.

In the governor's dining room was a delicious brunch. Mr And Mrs Dushe, Lilith, Starlight, the girls, and Mr Aroth were there. They were enjoying a funny talk and a nice breakfast. Starlight gave thanks to the governors for their hospitality, and for their support in the South Earth project. The time to go had come, and Starlight's farewell protocol took place in the castle. Aeda, Nemea, and Meletea wore beige, soft violet and aquamarine dresses embroidered with flowers. They had on precious long coats of the same colour as each respective dress. Their shoes were made of silver leather and embroidered with golden flowers. Starlight had on a turquoise imperial jacket embroidered with roses and golden swans. Lilith wore a beautiful beige coat decorated with small stains of black and golden colour.

All of them were walking towards the caravan cars on a red velvet carpet outside the castle. At both sides along the carpet, were the guards of the fortress riding their white horses. The guards wore their luxurious uniforms. They were elevating and crossing their swords over the guests. Starlight, the girls, and Mr Aroth entered the central car. General Stealth and Officer Flussman were coordinating the security scheme. A few minutes later, the caravan was moving towards the airport. All lanes of the principal highway of Blue-Ice City were closed allowing the passage of Starlight's caravan.

He was seeing through his car window, the cypresses on the hills and some constructions of white walls and turquoise roofs passing so fast.

Once they arrived at the airport, they descended from the cars and walked a few steps where immigration agents were waiting for them. Those agents checked Starlight's passport and then his friend's identifications as well. Then Starlight, Mr Aroth, and the girls boarded a private jet, which was there ready for them. The inside of that plane was luxurious. It had beige leather sofas and big dark wooden tables for living rooms. There were three waitresses for catering services. The plane took off and the orange sun was in the background.

They arrived at Befomet City and people there received them as heroes. After descending from the jet, Starlight and his friends made the corresponding immigration registration. They took one congress limousine.

General Stealth approached them and said, "My Lord, and ladies. I am going to coordinate your transportation security. My Lord, the emperor wants to see you in the castle."

"Well, thank you my friend," Starlight said to him.

Befomet City Airport building was like a silver ant. Its design was wonderful. Its structure was made of steel and its windows were of silver colour. There was a marvellous complex of highways near the airport.

People outside the main international arrival gate noticed Starlight was in the limousine. Soon, many police patrols made way for that diplomatic car. The helicopters of television channels wanted to broadcast Starlight's arriving at Befomet City from the air as well. The main highway of the city was closed. At both sides of that highway, there was a big crowd waving Black Earth flags. People were enjoying Starlight's limousine path as in a parade. They had a lot of glee throwing confetti into the air. Starlight was greeting everyone from his diplomatic car.

Three military attack helicopters were over the caravan. Suddenly, two of those choppers started flying so low.

"Hey, there are civilians here. They cannot fly at that distance," a youngster in the crowd said to another one.

"Yes, you are right my friend," he answered him.

The emperor was following the parade on television. He was sitting on a luxurious beige sofa in a spacious room decorated with ancient artworks. There were three guards behind him, who wore black formal dresses with black ties. The emperor wore his turquoise cape embroidered with yellow threads at its edges with rectangular shapes. He was dressed in a soft black sweater made of tiny flakes of precious gems (sapphires, and diamonds), and a trouser in the same colour. He had golden leather boots and had put on his helmet, which covered all his face. Some of his blond hair appeared from the bottom part of that helmet.

Clever boy, you are doing exactly what I want. I am going to give you the welcome, the emperor thought, whilst continuing watching the hologram screen.

Moments later, the limousine arrived at the castle. The fortress opened its main doors. Starlight's caravan stopped its travel, whilst the attack helicopters were suspended in the air. There was a big red carpet behind the palace's principal entrance. On it were the emperor, his security personnel, the guard, and the imperial press. Starlight descended from the limousine and walked to the maximum authority of Black Earth. Both made themselves a bow. Then, the emperor gave a big hug to Starlight.

They walked, talking about the complications of the trip towards Blue-Ice City. The journalists, guards, and soldiers were behind them.

In the castle were all senators, even Paulge, Raw, and Thade. They were seated on comfortable black leather chairs allocated in a big room decorated with beige marble statues. There, the emperor took the word.

"Today is a happy day for our society. An honourable young politician is here teaching us the value of the strength to face adversities. His courage facing the attacks, and his determination to defend the values of our social structure is a proof that he is the new politician that we need."

At that moment, everyone was applauding. The emperor continued, "Now, our Congress President has good news to tell us."

"Friends, I am here today to say to each one of you, there is a new hope for our world. I travelled across Black Earth to obtain the support for all its leaders to get the desired peace with South Earth."

For a while journalists, congressional representatives, guards, soldiers, even General Stealth were stupefied. The three senators that were against Starlight's ideology smiled with a happy expression on their faces. Then, journalists started raising their hands to ask for that determination.

Starlight continued, "Now, we need the approval of our congress. Then, I am going to travel towards South Earth to speak directly with the leader of that region."

At that moment, all the senators got up from their chairs and applauded him. Meletea, Nemea, and Aeda were watching the transmission on a hologram screen placed in the limousine.

"With a rain of applause, peace is killed," Nemea said.

Then, the emperor left some issues, and every senator started signing them. After it, the emperor raised his right arm and Starlight's left arm as well.

"The peace agreement peace agreement is signed, welcome to the new world, a peaceful world," the emperor said.

In another limousine, outside the castle, Miss Flussman was watching the transmission.

"What is that? This is the antithesis of our society. A law imposed by the congress without any referendum. What happened to Starlight? I feel as if he was like other politicians, following his own interests."

Suddenly, people started leaving from their houses in Befomet City applauding and waving flags of Black Earth. Soon, the same was occurring at all cities and towns of Black Earth. After the signing, Starlight went alone towards his house. He would travel towards South Earth the next day and he must take a rest before doing it.

Once Starlight had arrived at his home in the congress residence area, he felt some waves entering his body. He started hearing a noisy whistle, like a train honking. Starlight opened his eyes and saw a green field with some hills as background. The wind was so strong. There was a small house made of rustic materials like cut wooden logs and mud as well. The structure of that house was so simple. It had a gabled roof with a chimney. Its windows were rectangular and had a green colour from the mould. The only door of that house opened, then a beautiful woman appeared. She was dressed in a bright white tunic decorated with diamonds. She had queen shoes made of fabric with golden threads, which had fixed small turquoise agates. She ported a crown made of gold with red rubies on her head. A big white owl with red eyes was on her right shoulder. Starlight was amazed to see that pretty woman.

Versaria the witch, he thought.

Her long blonde hair was moving with the wind. Her aquamarine eyes were fixedly seeing Starlight, whilst she was approaching him. Suddenly, she stopped walking. "You have the knowledge, but do you really want to use it?" she said to him.

"I know you are the wisest witch in this universe. Are you going to illuminate my way? Could you help me?"

"You must not try to find the answer from me. Do it yourself, young Emperor."

"Yes, lady Versaria. I want to change all the universes."

"So be it, my Lord."

Suddenly, the white owl left, flying to Starlight. At its half-fly path, the bird crossed through a transparent fluid wall. Then, from the owl's tail left silver stardust.

Starlight was amazed seeing the bird approaching him. Once, the owl traversed the fluid wall, that bird changed its colour from white to black and its eyes from red to aquamarine. The big black owl posed on the congress chairperson's left shoulder. Then, that bird began tightening Starlight's beige imperial jacket with its claws.

Over his tearing clothes, was running his blue blood. The owl started absorbing Starlight by its claws, whilst he was shouting. Soon, a big amorphous black mass with the shape of a bird and man appeared from that mixture. At that moment, that monster opened its dragon wings, and it grunted so loud.

Starlight woke up with much sweat on his forehead. Then he dried it.

"I must end up with this."

He accommodated his pillow and returned sleeping again. Hours later, the sun of a new day entered through all the windows of Starlight's house. He got up from his bed, and his room phone rang. Starlight took the call.

"Hello."

A person on the other end of the phone said, "My Lord, I am Mr Mocheluo calling from the Lexabyssi building. My code is 10170576. Your parents are here."

"Oh perfect, please let them enter the guests room number three near Amon Room."

"Ok, my Lord. Could I help you with another theme?"

"Yes, please, that catering service prepares them breakfast. I will be there in a few minutes."

"So be it, my Lord."

"Thank you."

Then, Starlight went towards that guests chamber.

His adoptive parents were a kind couple. Starlight's mother had a white face, brown hair, and dark green eyes. His father had brown eyes and hair. Furthermore, he had precious cinnamon coloured skin.

Starlight appeared in that room. He had boots, a trouser, and an imperial jacket of black colour. Then, the complete family was sitting there on big and black leather sofas. There were three rectangular windows with their frames made in white wood. He took place at the left of the salon and his parents at the right.

They were enjoying the precious smell of pine leaving from the checkered wood floor. The room was kept by liberty and justice marble sculptures. Those statues were near two white columns, which had chapiters with shapes of roses. At that moment, the waitresses appeared with breakfasts carrying them on three small dark wooden tables, which were mobile. The black tie dressed girls started allocating the food on the main table for Starlight and his guests. Then, the waitresses left the room and Starlight broke the protocol.

"Thank you for coming. I miss you so much."

"Son, I am worried for you. Do you think this is a good idea?" Starlight's adoptive mother said.

"Yes mom, you do not worry about it."

"My fear is that all of this may be a trick. I am worried if all this was a curtain to start a war. I believe in you my love, but I do not trust in all those politicians."

"Woman leave him in peace. We know him. He is so smart. I believe in him," the father said.

Then, they continued talking a lot about Starlight's childhood histories. Almost an hour later, they finished their breakfast and got up from their chairs. The members of that family gave themselves a big hug. They desired that moment to be an everlasting time. Some tears left their eyes.

"You do not be sad. I am going to return in three days. Therefore, we are going to see each other again. I am going to call you by satellite phone. I must go now. I love you so much," Starlight said to them.

They hugged them again. At that moment, a young Starlight's assistant appeared.

"It is time, my Lord" he said to him.

The congress chairperson gave a last hug to his parents and left the building rounded by thirteen guards. He looked up at the sky and saw a clear cyan heaven. The clouds were transparent. Their edges were well-defined, like drawn by a tiny pen of white ink. Starlight felt so happy and gave thanks to the gods to see that new day.

CHAPTER TEN

Through the Shadows

Seven armoured black sports utility vehicles were in front of him. In the air there were three military attack helicopters flying near there. Then Starlight boarded in the third black vehicle placed in the queue of that caravan. The cars and the attack helicopters started their journey. They went along the principal highway of Befomet City, which was closed for the pass of the convoy. Starlight was seeing the city through his black car window, the posts passed so fast in front of his eyes. One of the choppers was leading the caravan, another was in the middle, and the last one was at the rear part. A few soldiers were at both lateral sides of those attack helicopters ready to shoot in case of any terrorist attack. The caravan arrived at the Befomet City Airport, where many people were waiting for Starlight. The convoy entered directly at one army runway where a private jet and two fighters were. Starlight descended from the black car after his guards did. The attack helicopters were still flying in the air. The congress president turned his head and saw a group of soldiers approaching. In that group was General Stealth.

"My Lord, some of my people are going to go with you for your protection."

"Well, my friend. I am according to that."

"Our agents in South Earth told us that everything is prepared for your meeting with the leader of that region."

"Thank you, for everything."

"I would like to go with you, but I received orders from the emperor, my Lord."

"General Stealth, you do not worry about it. In three days, I am going to be here. We are going to talk about military strategy and international policy."

Starlight gave him an ancient handshake with his index finger extended. The military did the same to close the energy circle.

The congress chairperson and the soldiers boarded the jet. Meanwhile, four soldiers went in couples at each one of the combat fighters. The engine of all those planes started sounding. Once in his private plane, Starlight was looking through the window. He was observing the city, the airport, General Stealth, and some soldiers with him on the ground. Suddenly the planes took off, the jet first and the fighters behind it. That trip would take seven hours, five from Befomet City towards the Black Earth border, and two more over South Earth territory.

Starlight was in his room on the jet starting to read a book called: *Opposite Poles, Policies and Negotiations.* Its author was Mr Malmo.

Six hours later, General Stealth was in his office at the Befomet City BESA military complex. He was reading some issues. Suddenly, his door was knocked.

"Come in," he said without looking at the door.

Five men wearing black suits entered there. General Stealth touched a button under his table.

One of those black suit men showed him an official gold plate.

"National security yard, this is a sixty-six code. You are under arrest by the disappearance of the emperor."

"What?" General Stealth replied.

"You must keep in silence; you do not mention anything in your defence now, except when you are questioned in court. The Empire gives you a lawyer if you do not have one."

The anger seized him, but he had enough calm to say anything.

"It is unnecessary, the panic button. Here is the order of the empire supreme attorney," another man in black said.

General Stealth was so upset but understood the situation. He just got up from his chair and went with them. They left that office, seeing his soldiers arrested by more men in black.

Throughout Black Earth media were on air Messrs Paulge, Thade, and Raw. They were giving an intervention. People were watching that transmission massively. Senator Thade took the word.

"Black Earth people, today it supposes that will be the happiest day of our land. Instead of it, we must inform that our Emperor has been kidnapped."

At that point, people started crying to watch that broadcast in all thirteen regions. Others put their hands on their heads because they could not believe it.

Senator Raw continued, "Our national security yard intelligence has serious evidence the intellectual author of this tragedy was the president of our congress."

Starlight's parents were watching the transmission; they were hugging themselves.

"That could not be possible! My little boy is innocent, pigs!" his adoptive father said.

Just then, their house door opened rowdy. Some men in black entered as in General Stealth's office.

"Who are you?"

"You must keep in silence; you do not mention anything in your defence now, except when you are questioned in court. The Empire gives you a lawyer if you do not have one."

"My little boy is innocent, pigs!" Starlight's father said to them.

Then, those men took the couple by force. Starlight's parents were being crawled on the floor of their house by those men. The hologram television screen still projected the intervention of the three senators in that empty living room.

The figure of Senator Paulge was on television saying, "The swords of justice will fall on all those who committed this abominable act."

Nearby, a black luxury sports car rolled so fast on an avenue of Befomet City. In the car's interior were Meletea and Nemea. The hologram phone of the young blonde girl was ringing.

"Hi, is this a secure line?" Nemea asked.

On the other end of the phone was Aeda.

"Yes, it is."

"Well, we are going to go towards the location meeting."

"Ok, I will wait for it."

"*D'accord,* we are going to go faster."

A few minutes later, the sports car arrived at the science laboratories of Beliar High School. There, Mr Aroth was with Aeda, and Starlight's other friends.

He took the word, "Fellas, we are being persecuted. Now, we are accused of being responsible for the emperor's kidnapping. Therefore, we are going to communicate between us using these hologram phones."

Mr Aroth gave each one there a hologram phone.

He continued, "We must find Starlight. We are one, as he says to us."

Each one there nodded.

"Yes, Mr Aroth you have the reason," Nemea said.

At that moment, another troop of men in black arrived at Amon Room. The congress representatives were in session except the senators: Paulge, Thade, and Raw.

"You must keep in silence; you do not mention anything in your defence now, except when you are questioned in court. The Empire gives you a lawyer if you do not have one," one of the black suit men said with a strong voice to the senators.

The representatives were not handcuffed by their diplomatic status. However, they were forced going towards the empire supreme attorney for their judgment. They were transported in armed patrols and not in their limousines.

Starlight left his book falling from his bed because he was asleep. Suddenly, an intense noise sounded. The two fighter guardians of Starlight's jet exploded. There were many explosive devices along their inner fuselage. A few seconds later, the congress president's plane exploded as well.

The jet started moving downwards, and some guards were floating as if there was no gravity.

That plane got in vertical position and then it descended in free fall. The guards were trying to hold on to something. However, they were launched out from the damaged jet one by one by the suction effect.

Then, the fuselage started giving many turns, whilst it was falling. Many things left it: papers, food, guns, and some parts of the jet. Starlight's bed was fixed at the plane's floor. He was holding himself from that furniture. The fuel of the jet was leaving with a spiral path towards the sky. An electric spark from a cable ignited the fuel and soon there was a big twist of fire above the falling jet.

Starlight could not hold for too long from his bed and was launched from the fuselage giving turns in the air. The panic made him vomit like in the first day of his fighter pilot classes. Starlight could see the fragments of the jet and the fire in that opaque heaven. He could not breathe so well and started getting a faint. His eyes were so white. Obstreperously, his body collided with the top part of a wood of many big and strange trees. Starlight just could see the sun's position during his falling.

"*Ny up, seed Morfim fee as not as* ..." he just could listen to a weak voice saying that, then he fainted.

Starlight impacted against the trees and his impulse made him traverse the branches of that vegetation as a projectile. The twigs cut him, and his blue blood left a trace. Nearby, the pieces of the jet in flames were falling among the trees. Far beyond, there were the fragments of the two fighters. The sun had a burgundy colour. The night was approaching and different species of animals and birds from that part of the planet started emitting their nocturnal sounds. At that moment, Starlight woke up, he could not move so well. Then, he saw his watch. Its crystal was fragmented, and its bezel broken. It was six-sixteen in the afternoon.

"*Oh, mein Gott*, I would like all this to be a dream." He continued his monologue, "Well, if I find survivors? Starlight, you must think please! It was a massacre, and I am alone in hostile territory."

At that moment, he started breathing so restlessly and leaving from his eyes were tears.

The creatures of that wild landscape continued making many noises. Starlight broke many tree branches trying to make way for himself. He moved so clumsily because he was so scared. The tree leaves were so big, wide, and prickly. The congress president slipped making much noise. His heart was beating so fast. *Oh Gott! The creatures of South Earth should not find me,* he thought.

Starlight felt embedded in an enormous piece of filth and mud, which was on the soil. His imperial jacket, boots, and trouser were torn up completely. Thereunder, that young man found his spider dress, which had been exhibited to General Stealth. Starlight put off his threadbare imperial clothes and put on his polymer dress in South Earth creature mode. That dress acted like a real costume of Agnesii race. It was to use in case of emergency or disappointments with South Earth people.

Starlight was approaching a big river, when he listened to some gasps and footsteps from many people. He was so scared and slipped again. Starlight fell in the river, which was as muddy as the soil. The upstream of the river carried him far from there towards the north. He could see some red and brilliant eyes of creatures running towards where he was. Suddenly, the young man felt something pulling his right foot in the water. Then, he was submerged into the river, whilst he activated the breathing device in his mouth. The polymer dress had that device incorporated.

Starlight saw his foot, there was one tentacle fixed there. He tried taking it off when another tentacle held his right hand. Other appendage appeared around his neck squeezing him so strong. Starlight was trying to loosen from them, but more tentacles trapped him faster. Soon, a face mix of a bat and a mantis appeared in front of that young man. The monster had big and semitransparent wings of violet colour. It had neither fins nor feet. It had eleven tentacles at each side of its long and big ant shape body.

The creature was the same size as Starlight. Its wings and appendages made it look quite greater than it was. The big, bizarre monster opened its jaws to devour Starlight. Suddenly in that place, appeared a whale shark with a reptile snout. It had a dark blue colour and white pigments. The movement of some algae behind the reptile-whale seemed as if that vegetation was moved by wind. The enormous reptile turned to the predator prey couple (Starlight and the strange, winged monster). The whale opened its jaws to eat the monster.

The reptile's teeth broke the mantis being into two parts leaving much dark green blood staining the water. At that moment, the winged monster released Starlight, and he could swim towards the surface. However, the whale reptile started pursuing Starlight as well. He saw a rift in a rock wall and held onto it.

Suddenly, the wall moved entirely. That enormous rock was not a wall. It was the back part of a giant grey reptile, which was quiet in the river. It had gross skin, scaly and sheer. Then, the new monster turned to see the whale fixedly. The whale went away scared because its size was smaller than its adversary was.

Meanwhile, Starlight continued hanging from the back of the grey reptile. The giant monster started walking into the river and a few minutes later, Starlight got loose from its back. He swam towards the surface following the light of the moon, which was entering through the water of the river. Starlight arrived at the riverbank wet and weak. He was so cold.

The moon was in a waning crescent and the stars on the firmament were so brilliant because there were no artificial lights. The shadow on the celestial vault made by the asteroid belt was reflecting on the entire South Earth.

Starlight started walking into the bushy wood. Alone in the darkness, the youthful wanderer stepped on something hairy. He saw a black stain on the soil. Starlight got scared and fell on his buttocks. He started crawling backwards. The young man found a wooden stick to touch the strange thing. He approached the stick and noted the hairy thing was a big and old fur of some animal maybe skinned by another one. Starlight put on that fur and looked for a cave to sleep in, because the night was each time colder.

He found one with a small entrance.

Thank you, gods. The entrance is small enough to let a big beast enter.

Then, Starlight entered it and caressed his feet, which were bleeding out. He never had walked barefoot. His blue blood was leaving a trace on the marshy soil.

At last, Starlight could sleep after all those events. However, he woke up scared many times during that night. Just the stars kept his dreams in that cold obscurity. Strange crows of three eyes looked at him without emitting any noise.

A few hours later, a great shine appeared over Starlight's eyelids. He opened his blue eyes and saw an orange sun, which illuminated all that area. Starlight woke up trying to remember where he was and who he was. That young man did not remember anything until his brain started setting up. A moment later, he came to himself and understood the situation again. His mind wanted to erase that episode from him, but the new reality came so fast.

Then, Starlight left the cave.

The appearance of his polymer attire was brawny but some fat. His skin was grey and solid as a rock. The top part of his feet were like claws, his hands and head were his own. Starlight's feet continued bleeding out. That situation did not matter to him because he just wanted to take away his sadness and find the leader of South Earth.

Soon, the brilliant orange sun was taking its natural grey colour. In that part of the planet, the days had a few minutes of sunlight. Starlight had not activated the hands and head cover of his costume yet. It was because the attire would make him sweat a lot on his face and hands. He just continued walking under the grey sky.

The days passed in the same way for Starlight. He was walking alone through the shadows, drinking some pestilent water, and sleeping in caves. Meanwhile, in

Black Earth the chaos was reigning. The sovereigns of that place were the senators: Paulge, Thade, and Raw. The tyranny for Hur-Appean people had come. Troops of soldiers were arriving at the laboratories of Royal Imperium University and Beliar High School. The new military personnel were confiscating everything there: papers, experiments, and equipment. They were following the orders of the three senators. The new government had abolished the congress and had undertaken all The emperor's affairs as well.

Senator Thade took the leadership of the instigating trio. The three tyrants were in the Tartarusm Square in front of a military parade.

"Fellows, this is the new order of our society. We are the water that is going to clean our land from any peace enemy. Long live the new Empire!" Mr Thade said to the new soldiers.

"Long live the new Empire!" the soldiers said to him, raising their right arms.

"Boys, go for them," the senator said.

At that moment, behind the congress buildings appeared many military attack helicopters and fighters flying towards South Earth. The thirteen cities of Black Earth were militarized. There was much rowdyism due to the tyranny and the new political regime. Police and army were at the service of the new government and had orders to arrest or execute any rebel, civilian, or military who was against the new government. For that reason, many of Starlight's friends were in jail.

Besides, many soldiers patrolled the cities, and others marched in squadrons towards South Earth. The three senators had ordered conquering that territory.

Meanwhile, the ex-congress president continued walking towards the main city of South Earth. On his way, Starlight felt so tired. He found a big and rotten wooden log behind a bush and sat down on it. He took a rest and started falling asleep. Among some branches of the bush, Starlight saw himself dressed in a royal manner seated on a bench.

"Why did you betray me?" he asked his own image.

The doppelgänger had a scared face and just could answer, "I never had betrayed you."

Starlight for the first time activated the hands and face of his South Earth costume. The face of the attire was grey and deformed, whilst his eyes were entirely black. His body, even his head, were still covered by the black fur. Starlight seemed a death shadow and continued seeing his own double settled on the bench. The rover young man walked towards that park chair and then he kissed his replica. The doppelgänger disappeared, and the nomad Starlight was alone in that strange landscape. Then, he started to cry.

Just then, Starlight understood the strange presence that he felt during his life was always himself. Then, Starlight left his own thoughts and took a second wind to continue his way towards the fortress' leader of South Earth.

Many days later, he arrived at that location. Starlight could see the main construction of South Earth and its surroundings. The houses of the creatures were caves, and the bastion leader was a dark massive castle. At its bottom, there were enormous gates. Inside, a light was produced by a big fire. Magma rivers were making way among the caves. There were mud and the dead bodies of animals and South Earth creatures.

The Agnesii used the magma to forge their weapons and cook their food. Their nourishment was the dead animals and bodies of their own race stacked outside of their caves. All magma rivers converged in the fortress gates. At that moment, Starlight arrived at that entrance. *How am I going to enter there? How to know, where is the leader?* he thought.

The castle had at its centre a massive and tall tower. At its upper part, there was a big gargoyle made of stone. From its snout left flames, which made that construction look more impotent.

Starlight continued walking towards the entrance and picked up from the ground a dead creature. Then, he carried it on his back. There, many creatures were working, carrying food for their leader. The pestilent odour, the dead creature, and his costume let Starlight walk and enter the fortress without any problem.

The youthful wanderer was so amazed to see the interior of that place with his black eyes. The fortress was enormous and there were squadrons of creatures armed and training for a single combat. At first, Starlight believed they were snarling, but he noted they could speak as well.

Starlight had not been so scared in his life. He ascended some black stairs, which were in that fortress. South Earth creatures were in a queue there. Then, he arrived at the mid part of the tower. He left from the line and then, he got entered the fortress. Starlight found a dark corridor and opened a black door.

At the other side, was an illuminated room. It seemed a place as a part of Black Earth, but located in South Earth. There were many candles, a black grand piano, and some sculptures as well. Starlight saw a black silhouette of a man, which seemed to be wearing a helmet and a cape. His head covering was made of gold with slots of turquoise colour for his eyes and nose.

"Emperor, what is all this?" Starlight said, amazed.

"My boy. I was so sure that you would arrive here. Now, I corroborate my thoughts. In fact, I was prepared for your visit…"

"Why are you here?" Starlight interrupted him obfuscated.

"Not, boy. The real question is, what are you here?"

"What? I just want to get peace between Black and South Earth. I came here and found you. Oh, *mein Gott.* Are you the leader?"

"The important question is who are you? Why did you travel here? Do you know all about the events in the past? Wake up! You had been in a bottle. You must know the truth or suffer the consequences of your ignorance."

Starlight thought that his life was in a risky situation. He looked at another door and ran and left that room. A few seconds later, two South Earth creatures entered where their leader was.

"You already know what to do," the emperor said to them.

"Yes, my Lord."

Starlight ran as fast as he could, avoiding meeting with the natives. In a miracle situation he could leave the fortress and hide in the dark wood.

The night had fallen, and the vagabond was being pursued by thirty-three creatures and thirteen monsters as dogs. Those animals had three heads of bats without ears. They had fur just on their backs, their skin was grey, and their eyes were red. Those dogs were sniffing so fast with their bat noses to find the sweaty odour of Starlight.

CHAPTER ELEVEN

Amazon Luciferin

The way was darker, and Starlight could not see a gulch, which was near him. He fell giving many turns. His fall had stopped due to the muddy terrain. Starlight just saw his persecutors and their dogs running at the top part of that gulley. Soon, two brilliant yellow eyes appeared behind him. A black claw with large nails caught Starlight. It dragged him over the muddy brush. Suddenly, the rover was in front of a South Earth creature. Starlight was so scared. The monster was holding him by his right leg. The creature was like Starlight's costume. A dark skin, few hairs, big horns, a great forehead, and brawny. Its voice was guttural and squeaky.

"What is your name?" that creature asked.

Starlight just could feel fear and distrustfulness.

"I am Gotrigch, and we can be friends if you want. Why are they pursuing you?"

Starlight remained silent.

"I live far from the fortress and have read some books…"

At that moment, Starlight broke his stillness.

"Books?"

"Yes, I know there are few of us that like reading…"

The monster moved its bat nose. Starlight realised the monster believed that he was another creature. However, Gotrigch had discovered him. Starlight was scared again.

hit it with a rock near him, he thought

Nevertheless, he decided to continue with the conversation.

"Where are the books?"

The monster looked at him in an inquisitive manner.

"Now, I understand. You are different, but you should not worry. I noted that you are from Black Earth."

Starlight was petrified. He thought the monster wanted to kill him.

The creature continued, "I am against the hatred between two races. You should be unafraid for me. Your real enemies are there, above."

"I am Starlight. Where did you read the books?"

"The books are scarce and sub estimated. I thought you did not know about South Earth's history."

Starlight's mood changed from fear to curiosity.

"Really not," he said.

"There was a time where a member of the Black Earth Royal family came towards these strange lands with his friends. They were militaries and scientists as well. They wanted to explore and colonise these lands. They brought with them a new race made in the laboratory. That race was us. Those Hur-Appeans made us under rules of cryobiology. We were in peace until the day that another fraction of Black Earth amry came here to eradicate us. They changed our DNA, transforming us into this."

"Gotrigch, you have not answered me yet," Starlight said to him.

"Yes, the books are in the Sattrin Tower."

Starlight understood the tower was the same fortress where he was.

"Have you got access to them?"

"No, I have not for now. I outwitted the security a few years ago. However, it is so difficult now."

"Well, you said to me that Black Earth army changed your DNA. Right?"

"Yes, they arrived at this territory with many scientists guided by the lord of the gargoyles. The books said that a great Agnesii died trying to make us free. His name was Be Alpha Men who fought against the Hur-Appean army."

Starlight was amazed, but he did not say anything about it.

The monster continued, "I called them books, but they are papyrus. A lot of them were destroyed in the war. For that reason, they are not complete now."

At that time, some branches sounded.

"My friend, we must move. I think the rest of Sattrin Tower is still looking for you."

"Well, come on," Starlight said.

So, the rover and his new friend left there walking through the tropical woods. They walked all night until they found a few caverns to take a rest. From those caves they could see the infinite stars of the celestial vault. The vegetation had a strange and natural decoration of neon multi-colour lights. Those illuminations were everywhere and floating on air as well.

"This is the first time in my life that I have seen the Amazon Luciferin," Starlight said.

"What did you see?" the monster asked.

"The vibrio and the pyrocystis. They are bright bacteriums, which grow in jungle environments. They help to decompose the dead vegetation in the soil or water."

"Here they called the Panchea," Gotrigch said to him.

The conversation ended there. Both Starlight and the creature started sleeping in the caverns.

The next day, the orange sunshine crashed against Starlight's black eyes. Gotrigch would guide his new friend to return towards Black Earth. Starlight dawned that Gotrigch just ate fruits and branches. He started eating the same as his South Earth friend.

Almost three months later, on a common day the fog was ascending through the air covering the soil. The big tropical vegetation contrasted with the moor weather. That day, Starlight and the creature were traversing a swamp. There were muddy rocks along all that landscape. The travellers were advancing snuggled (to avoid falling in the pestilent green water). Starlight saw many strange insects in the water, whilst he was crawling. Soon, the man and monster reached the mainland.

The soil started trembling, whilst they were sitting there. Suddenly, from that terrain left many grey giant wetas and black and green flies, which had a size of one of Starlight's hand. Then, he turned his head to see Gotrigch.

"It is normal?"

"No, this just happened when a great trooper of snuchkurls and their owners get approaching," Gotrigch answered.

"Yes, the big hunting dogs that were behind me the day that I met you."

Gotrigch interrupted him, "Yes… or when there is a flood."

Starlight was scared.

"So, what do we do?"

"Just run."

At that moment, they started running. The soil each time trembled with more frequency.

Starlight and Gotrigch were shooing the flies and giant wetas away. The insects were trying to enter by the mouths of those two peers. Suddenly, Gotrigch and Starlight were rounded by a squadron of Agnesii warriors that had arrived there.

Starlight was still wearing his South Earth bio attire and the animal fur on his back. He never let Gotrigch see his face. The Agnesii troop each time was closer. Gotrigch looked at Starlight.

"It is good to die near a friend."

"Today is not a day to die," Starlight said.

So, that couple of rovers started fighting with all those creatures. The monster warriors had weapons and the wanderer explorers just their defence abilities. Starlight was turning on a button of his costume. It was for the transparency effect. However, that system on his clothes was damaged. It made Starlight seem like a ghost instead of a transparent being. Then, he appeared giving a punch here and at another instant giving a kick there. At that moment, a great noise sounded and all Agnesii turned their heads and started running randomly.

"What is that?" Starlight asked Gotrigch.

"A flood."

Therefore, the Black Earth vagabond and his friend ran towards the trees to climb them so fast. The water started razing everything in its path. Starlight was on the top part of his tree seeing the flood. A giant weta flew to him and started walking on his face. However, that young man continued, petrified, seeing how the trees fell by the force of the water. Soon, his tree fell and Gotrigch's as well.

Those two partners were dragged by the stream until they arrived at the top of a precipice. In that place there was a cliff, and the water was descending from it. The two peers were on the edge of that precipice. Gotrigch was seeing Starlight, who was hanging about to fall. The creature made a strange smile and then gave him its hand. The monster helped the young Hur-Appean man to climb. Starlight was so amazed.

"Thank you, friend."

Gotrigch continued smiling. Then, it turned its head and saw many Agnesii that were running to them. Gotrigch turned its head and looked at Starlight again.

"Friend, you run and find your way," it said to its partner.

Then, Gotrigch ran to Agnesii horde and started fighting with them. Starlight got up, but he slipped and fell.

He just could scream, "Gotrigch!"

Then, everything was in darkness. On the river stream it could see some dead Agnesii, insects and pieces of trees. Suddenly, on that same river was reflected a shadow of a flying gargoyle. That wide waterway was called the Appyllonium River. It had a gorgeous path through the tropical wood. At the end of its way towards the north, it found the Olympus Sea. The river formed a magnificent falls system, which was on the natural wall. It was because South Earth was elevated from the continental shelf. That natural wall was the same that Starlight saw with Lilith from Blue-Ice City. The Olympus Sea divided the Black and South Earth.

On the beach of the north border was crawling a strange being. He was a young man with many wounds. His dark blue blood was staining the white velvet beach sand. That being on the seashore was Starlight. He arrived at the border of the Eschem Region. There, he was so happy to find the military guard.

"Help me!" he just could say with a weak voice.

The guards saw him crawling. However, they waited for him until his arrival.

"Bugger. Where do you think you are going?" one of the guards said to him.

"I am Starlight," he just could babble.

"Fellows, that rat can speak," the guard turned his head and said to his peers.

Then, the guard kicked Starlight's stomach.

The wounded young man writhed in pain.

"I am Starlight."

Another military guard was eating a long elongated white bread. He got up from his chair and approached Starlight as well.

The military pronounced with a Fleuretty Region accent, "This fool insect. Although someone lets you speak? Retard! These aliens from South Earth just need a good beating as an animal. I am going to give you four hundred hits."

Then, the guard started hitting Starlight with a wooden rod.

The young and wounded man continued until faint.

"I am Starlight. I am Starlight."

The night had come and after the beating the guards took Starlight towards the dungeon of the border station.

The three senators in Befomet City were informed that someone was captured near the South Earth border and his name was Starlight. Therefore, they wanted to corroborate his identity to be imprisoned. Immediately, the three senators gave the order to take the suspect from the border towards the main military base of the Eschem Region.

Starlight was allocated by the soldiers in a dark and wet dungeon infested with rats. He fell asleep there after the beating. The bed of that place was made of concrete, and it had neither a pillow nor blankets.

One hour later, Starlight woke up due to the bites of the rodents. His blood continued running over his naked body. He tried getting up, but he slipped in a puddle of pestilent water in his cell. At the right side of the bed was a nasty toilet without water. It was full of filth until its edge. Starlight was holding from that latrine to slip not again. At that moment, a black dressed military man and four regular soldiers arrived at the dungeon.

"My superiors said to me that here… is someone called Starlight," the black dressed military said to the rover.

The naked and wounded young man got up.

"I am Starlight!" he said vigorously, but with a weak voice.

"Take him. The supreme leaders want him alive. Then, we must focus on the war. For the victory!" the leader of those militaries exclaimed.

The rest of those soldiers said as well, "For the victory!"

What war? Are we at war? What is going on here? Starlight thought.

The one soldier opened the cell, and the rest entered there and took Starlight, dragging him. Then, he would be transported in a military lorry.

The wounded young rover was still nude. On his face, there were pieces of filth from the dungeon toilet and many stains of his blue blood. On the lorry the soldiers continued giving him a great beating. Starlight tried defending himself without success.

A tropical storm started falling there, and the drops of rain decorated the inter-regional highway. Soon, an intense sound of a fly was coming near the military vehicle. The soldiers on the lorry paid no attention to that noise, they continued beating Starlight. In fact, one of them held to the rover, whilst the others continued hitting him. The military who was holding the ex-president of the congress had his right arm rounded the young prisoner's neck. However, that same soldier put an explosive device on the metallic wall of the lorry with his left hand.

Suddenly, he launched himself together with Starlight to the hauler floor. A second later the device exploded, that fact deconcentrated to the driver making the armoured lorry give many turns. The soldiers were crashing against the vehicle walls. Once the hauler stopped, some soldiers were dead in the military vehicle. The others were expelled from the lorry through the opened back doors. The young man and his benefactor soldier continued glued to the floor of the transportation. It was because the military who took Starlight had a glove with a magnetic device that let him be fastened to the metallic floor of the vehicle. Then, Starlight and that soldier stood up leaving from the damaged lorry.

Outside, a black sports car with the shape of a bat arrived (its motor made the fly sound). Starlight looked at it scared with his blue eyes. The right door of that car opened in a vertical way. In the car was a white girl with black hair as the night and grey eyes. She was amazed seeing her friend so thin, dirty, and hurt.

"My Lord…" she said to Starlight.

He was so happy to see that girl.

"Meletea, my darling."

A wounded soldier at the senator's service got up holding a weapon pointing to Starlight. Then, that military shot his gun. At the same time, Starlight's rescuer shot at the senator's soldier. The military footman of the new regime fell dead to the ground. The brown-haired and blue-eyed soldier who had helped Starlight to leave the lorry turned to see the ex-congressman.

"For the victory, my Lord."

Then, he fell dead by the flunkey's bullet.

Starlight left some tears from his eyes.

"For the victory, my friend."

"My Lord, he was one of our most loyal friends. Now, we must focus. Time is running out," Meletea said to Starlight.

"Yes, lady Meletea."

Meanwhile, two black sport utility cars were approaching there. Two soldiers descended from each sport utility car. They were Meletea's guards. Then, Starlight and the girl went towards the sports car.

The soldiers that came from SUVs carried the military body loyal to Starlight towards one of the black utility cars. Once they put the body in the back part of the vehicle, they started following Meletea's car.

The drops of rain continued falling in a diagonal direction. Starlight was looking at nothing through that car window.

"My Lord, you put on this uniform," Meletea said to him.

He put on that military clothing.

"Thank you, my lady. Really, this is a dream come true. Be here on safe hands again. Why do you wear a normal jacket instead of a coat?"

"My Lord, everything has changed, absolutely nothing is the same here."

Starlight got worried again, whilst he saw many fighters in the dark sky.

"We are at war, my Lord. Messrs Paulge, Thade, and Raw abolished the congress," Meletea said to him.

"Lady Meletea, I am to take charge of all this. I need a meeting with the rest of the girls, Mr Aroth, Captain Thunder, and General Stealth. And… my parents… are they alright?"

"I am sorry my Lord. They are under arrest in Befomet City jail."

At that moment, the neck of Starlight started changing shape. It was like an insect under his skin.

"You have not to worry about it, my Lord. We are going to rescue them. The Teenage Rebel Minds," Meletea said to him.

"Who is your leader?"

"You, my Lord."

"So be it."

"Now, you should go to the doctor first."

She took Starlight's hands and continued, "We are going to take a fighter and then to go to the safest place in the world. The secret basements of Royal Imperium University."

At that moment, the caravan went off the road towards an area of big bushes. They covered a military chopper. The rain was still falling so hard, whilst many other attack helicopters and Death Angels in the sky were flying towards the border.

The caravan stopped and the soldiers descended from SUVs. Then, they put explosives in those cars. They made the same with the bat shaped sports car. Those militaries loyal to Starlight activated the automatic pilots of each vehicle. Then, they took the body of the dead soldier. They wrapped it in a large cloth and carried it to the helicopter.

Starlight, Meletea, and their guards boarded the chopper as well. That combat machine left from that place furrowing the sky so fast. A few minutes later, the bat shaped car and the SUVs exploded.

Meletea's military helicopter arrived at one secret air military base in a sierra of sedimentary rocks a few hours later. There were many soldiers faithful to Starlight. The people were celebrating the arrival of their leader. The surprise of everyone to see him so thin and battered did not remove the happiness of those military men and women. Soon, a white soldier with precious slanted eyes approached Starlight.

"It is an honour to meet you, my Lord."

"The honour is mine."

"For the victory!" the soldier said to him with glee.

The people there started acclaiming.

"For the victory!"

A sensual military black girl approached Starlight as well.

"My Lord, we need you to create peace here again," she said to him.

The young man put his hands on the military girl's arms looking at her fixedly.

"I am going to do that."

"Thank you, my Lord. Welcome, peace creator," she said to him.

Then, the rest of the people cheered, "Welcome, peace creator. Welcome, peace creator."

Starlight opened so wide his amazed eyes to listen to them.

"*Grata ad solis ortum*," he said to himself.

A military lorry arrived there. It was an ambulance without sirens. That car would provide medical service to Starlight. Very few military servicemen knew about the secret base under the Imperial University buildings. All of them were loyal to Starlight.

"The emperor knows about my location?" Starlight asked.

Meletea lowered her head and looked at the floor.

"My Lord, the emperor is dead."

Starlight was surprised.

"My lady. I need to talk with you after my recovery," he said to his friend.

"So be it, my Lord."

Meletea and the paramedics accompanied Starlight towards the lorry. That ambulance left that hidden military base towards the inner of the sierra. Starlight was so happy to see the shine of freedom again. Then, a military paramedic put an oxygen mask over Starlight's face and said, "My Lord. I am going to give you a sedative under your permission."

Starlight held Meletea's right hand.

"Go on, my friend."

Then, the paramedic activated a white dispenser and a semitransparent gas appeared into the mask. At the same time, the paramedic was giving him IV fluids. The liquid entered through the left arm of the rebels' leader. The paramedic was amazed by the blood colour of Starlight. Then, the Black Earth leader closed his eyes.

Days later, Starlight woke up in a room of soft grey colour. He was in a kind of clinical room. His bed was between two pools of warm water. There was steam leaving from them. There was a goat head hanging from one of the walls there. He saw himself and noted he had a lot of needles stuck in his skin. Three soldiers were guarding the entrance of that room. They were outside the room. Aeda, Nemea, and Meletea arrived there. The soldiers let them enter.

Once into the room the girls said, "Good morning, my Lord."

Starlight was so happy to see them, and the girls were pleased as well. They tried kissing him avoiding the needles.

"Good morning, my friends. How long have I been asleep?"

"Six days, my Lord," Nemea answered him.

"Well, it is time to wake up." Starlight tried getting up from his bed. However, he could not do that.

"My Lord, you try taking a rest. Your muscles are still in recovery," Aeda said to him.

"I am so happy, because I know your face," Starlight interrupted her and continued, "My young ladies. What is the purpose of this pleasant visit?"

Aeda took the word again.

"We, your real friends, are representatives from Royal Imperium University and people loyal to you. The proposal of this visit is seeing you guiding our people. See you as the emperor that you must be, my Lord."

"Well, it is an interesting proposal. As a plant is irrigated with sunlight and water. Friendship must be irrigated with confidence and love."

Again, the girls gave a kiss on Starlight's forehead and said goodbye leaving from that room.

CHAPTER TWELVE

The Return of Starlight

Alone in that room Starlight closed his blue eyes. His K-complex made some explosions on his thoughts. He felt strange waves entering his body. Then, Starlight saw himself at the top part of a pyramid of Agnesii dead bodies. He was upon those bodies so proud and victorious. Soon, a black hand left the pick of that pile of lifeless creatures. That claw had long and dirty nails. Then, an arm and a head appeared. It was Godrigch's head. It was looking at Starlight.

"*Omnia Est Unum*," the monster said to him.

Starlight woke up with his throat so dry and his forehead wet from his sweat. He saw the roof of the room and denoted the shadow of a gargoyle.

"*Zen sheer naa wop yub loose am*," he said to himself.

Day by day military doctors removed the needles from Starlight's skin. Months later, he recovered successfully. At the end of that long process, Starlight was ready to go towards his own new room. The university's basement was a bunker, and all its rooms had grey walls and metallic doors like a submarine.

Starlight would take his first breakfast on a table after much time. He entered a dining room full of soldiers. That area connected with a kitchen and a corridor. Starlight realised Officer Flussman was there.

He ran to give her a big hug.

"Heissel, is nice to see you again."

She was amazed because the ex-president congress called her by her first name.

"My Lord, is nice to see you alive."

Then, two old friends of Starlight entered. The first one was a man with short blond hair and green eyes, he was Captain Thunder. Behind him, entered General Stealth. Starlight gave them a big hug.

"My Lord, it is so great you are here with us again," General Stealth said to him.

"My Lord, it is time that you guide our people again," Captain Thunder said.

"Yes, captain," Starlight answered.

"Ladies, gentlemen, leave us with Mr Starlight and the captain alone," General Stealth said to everyone.

They left there, and the room just sheltered Starlight and the two military men. They sat down and started talking.

General Stealth took the word.

"My Lord, people preferred being in their houses to avoid misunderstandings with the military regime. The servicemen of the new government were arresting every suspecting person in each city of Black Earth. In fact, Captain Thunder and I were in jail. Fortunately, we could escape, but more innocents like your parents are still there. That scenario made all people start meeting in the drainage systems to create: the resistance. That subversive group was joined with the Rebel Teenager Minds. The idea is to overturn the new government."

Starlight took a big breath.

"Well, it is time to face my destiny. I am going to bring freedom to my people."

Outside of the bunker, the sky was blue, and the edges of the clouds seemed painted with a tiny brush with white ink. The whole clouds were transparent, and the sun was so shiny.

Three months after the talking between Starlight, Messrs Stealth, and Thunder, many militaries loyal to General Stealth arrived at the basement for a meeting in a secret way. Aeda, Nemea, and Meletea were in that assembly as well. A few minutes later, Starlight was in front of those people. He was behind a Venician atrium made of marble with two columns, which ended in chapiters. On their base was a plate with the inscription:

Beati luce.

It was a replica of the atrium located in the Tartarusm Square.

Starlight started giving a speech with a strong voice. "Fellows, during the last months each one of us had passed many hard events. Those situations had affected our families, our lives, and the destiny of our land. The last weeks we have received total support from our people to develop an ambitious plan to recover our freedom. All these last days we are training, creating the military strategy, and taking our technological advances in our favour. I am not saying this could be easy. However, today we are not going to yield in front of any tyrant. Go forward, for the victory."

There, all the people were applauding him.

"For the victory!" they replied.

Then, all of them started running towards white spaceships called Dragonflies by their shape. The pilots with their airships started leaving from there by tunnels. They had their exits in a hills system so far from the emperor's castle. In the deepest deck of the university's basement was the central control of the rebel troops. That base was operated by Mr Aroth.

The Dragonflies left Befomet City area towards the south border of Black Earth. At that moment, a big thunder fell from the black sky of the South Earth. Starlight saw it from his airship and said to himself, "Fear not to the distant storm."

Remembering the image of Lilith, Starlight continued his monologue, "No one has seen her in a long time. So, I am going to find her. For the moment, I must be concentrated in the battle for the freedom of this land."

Once the rebel's airships arrived at the border between the two subcontinents, some Death Angels behind them were ready to shoot. At that moment, a second thunder fell.

Suddenly, a part of the natural wall of the South Earth border exploded. From that hole, left thousands of Agnesii armoured with rustic shields and axes. They were running so fast towards the beach at the Black Earth side. They could not swim. However, some of them could pass the ocean over the dead bodies of the other Agnesii who tried crossing the sea first.

"This is so easy. Boys, on my mark. Fire!" one pilot of the new government said.

All the Death Angels started to shoot at the creatures. Nevertheless, the Agnesii arrived at the Black Earth side.

"Fire on the ground," one blond military man said in a tank by his helmet microphone.

Instantly, all armoured tanks of the new regime started shooting at the creatures on the beach.

Starlight was still in his Dragonfly suspended in the air. He had a pilot helmet with a black visor.

"Hold on," he just said it on his communication device.

The Dragonflies around Starlight's airship were suspended as well. Those aircrafts had a spherical semitransparent shield, which protected them from the shots of the tanks and the Death Angels.

The creatures were advancing on the beach and starting to destroy the tanks. The new regime's bullets and torpedoes did not damage the Agnesii. At that moment, a third thunder fell in the natural wall. From there, more monsters left ready to kill anything in their path.

Starlight gave an order with a strong voice, "Fire!"

The Dragonfly airships started shooting blue lights. Those rays could cut and destroy the shields of Agnesii and kill them as well. One of the militaries in one chopper gave the order.

"Withdrawal!"

The government fighters and the tanks marched backwards, whilst Starlight's airships continued shooting at the Black Earth enemies. The Dragonflies were advancing without entering South Earth territory.

The news channels were transmitting the battle. The three senators were watching those events on the hologram television screens in the Amon Room.

At that moment, Senator Paulge exclaimed, "Itis time to finish him!"

"How did he get that technology? If we have all his research projects," Senator Raw said.

"Fellows do not worry. Now, we must focus on these events. Listen! Now we have an alibi. We are going to send some nuclear capsules and obliterate the problem once for all," Senator Thade said.

Mr Raw took the word again.

"Yes, our alibi is imperial security."

"Perfect, we are going to start the phase: Erase-All. However, we must show the public that we are benevolent. *Panem et circenses*," Senator Paulge said laughing.

"It is correct, estimated senator," the other two old men said, smiling mockingly as well.

Meanwhile, Starlight and his pilots continued shooting at the Agnesii in the border.

"My Lord. Why do we not enter towards South Earth territory?" a pilot girl of another Dragonfly asked.

"My lady. We are here to protect our people, not to commit a genocide," Starlight answered her using his microphone.

"Yes, my Lord."

Suddenly, tanks and fighters loyal to the government turned and started shooting at the Dragonflies again. Starlight's airships had the spherical gel shield activated, which protected them from any attack. They were receiving all impacts from the bullets and torpedoes of the Black Earth army.

Officer Flussman was in another Dragonfly.

"My Lord, I will cover you," she said to Starlight using her microphone helmet.

"My lady, friends, please do not shoot at our people. We must continue defending our land. Move on, fellows!" Starlight said.

"Roger that," the rest of his pilots answered.

Just then, one Death Angel arrived at the battlefield. That fighter left a big torpedo. Instantaneously, the Death Angel retired from its trajectory going upwards. The torpedo was travelling between the fighters, choppers, and Dragonflies. Their objective was to impact the border beach.

Mr Aroth who was in the base of Starlight's army took his microphone and contacted the ex-congress president.

"My Lord, our system detected a nuclear ogive approaching the border."

"I got it," Starlight answered him.

Then, the young leader changed his intercommunication device.

"Captain Thunder, General Stealth."

"Yes, my Lord," both the captain and general answered from the other side.

"I am going to take the missile that is approaching me. That is a nuclear bomb. Once I get it, I am to fly upwards to avoid it exploding here."

"My Lord," General Stealth said.

"My Lord, this is a suicide way," Captain Thunder replied.

"Friends, it does not matter. I will not let my people die."

"So be it, my Lord," the two rebel militaries answered him.

The rest of Dragonflies were shooting at the invading creatures and avoiding the impacts from the troops of the Black Earth army.

Starlight piloted his airship towards the arriving nuclear ogive. The Hur-Appeans leader's Dragonfly could reorient the missile. It was because Starlight's airship had a special system of attraction. Once he had the control of the ogive, his Dragonfly started flying upwards. That airship was leaving from the silver troposphere and was entering the dark mesosphere of Sattrin Earth.

Starlight could see some stars as infinitesimal bright points and started feeling dizzy and somnolent.

On soil, at the rebel headquarters, Mr Aroth dropped his microphone to see the brave action of his master. The girls, Aeda, Meletea, and Nemea were in combat on air and each one dropped a tear for Starlight.

Officer Flussman closed her precious brown eyes.

For my Lord, she thought holding her Dragonfly stick.

She started shooting at any Agnesii and did it with much rage. Messrs Thunder and Stealth were seeing the laser network on the battlefield and the nonsense of the war. At one side of the natural wall, thousands of creatures continued crossing the border over the dead bodies of their mates. At the other side were the Dragonflies, Death Angels, soldiers, and armoured tanks shooting at those Agnesii.

Meanwhile, Starlight was seeing the stars and the asteroid belt almost unconscious.

What a wonderful universe, he thought.

Starlight turned off the system of attraction from his Dragonfly. Then, he activated a blue button on his pilot dress. After that, Starlight fainted in his spaceship, which was falling towards the Pandemonical Continent.

The ogive left the orbit of Sattrin Earth and continued floating towards the asteroid belt in a random way. That nuclear missile touched a space rocket exploding and causing a massive sinusoidal wave destroying a vast part of the asteroid belt.

From the border, both Agnesii and Hur-Appeans saw that big sparkle in the sky and then, many lines of fire in the heavens. Those were the fragments of asteroids entering Sattrin Earth.

One of the creatures that was still on the wall took a big horn. That instrument was made of a golden metal. It had figures of gargoyles sculpted on its exterior. The strange artefact was the Sattrin Horn, which produced a finite amount of sound enabled to be heardat a great distance. An interesting characteristic of the horn was that it needed an infinite quantity of gold to paint it. After the creature made that horn to sound, all Agnesii started returning towards their sub-continent side. They did it as fast as they entered Black Earth territory. Again, most of them died trying to cross the Olympus Sea from the Black Earth beach.

The wave of the ogive's explosion reached Starlight's Dragonfly. That airship started breaking, whilst its fuselage rubbed against the air. At the stratosphere, his aircraft had disappeared completely. The ex-congress chairperson's dress transformed into a golden biomechanical armour. It was because Starlight had activated the blue bottom.

In the sky, that luminous winged gargoyle was travelling in a downwards way as a falling bolt of blazing gold. The armour had long legs, eagle claws, and a man's face with horns.

"*Ny up, seed Morfim fee as not as,*" Starlight said with a guttural voice.

In another location of the universe, was the Nymph's headquarters. That fortress had many rooms, passages, and various underground levels. On its deepest deck, there was a box of silver and gold colour with many figures hewn on it. In that fortress, there was a dragon-demon keeping that mythological box. The cubical container had inside a silver flux, which was the dust of the existence origin. That place was rounded by columns, which ended in chapters as the head of the keeper monster. Near that pyxis, there was a room where Lilith was seated on a golden chair. It had many embedded emeralds. In that room were other Nymphs at Lilith's service.

"My queen, he is alive," one of them said to Lilith.

"I must resolve this," she answered.

Then, Lilith got up and gave an order, "Prepare me the portal."

"Yes, my queen."

A silver spaceship arrived at Lilith's fortress. There, she took that transportation and went towards the outside of the planet. That orb was a great mixture of green jungles and cities with dynamic skyscrapers. There were dome constructions and flying autos went in perfect order by air in those cities.

Once Lilith got to arrive at the exosphere of her planet, the lean design spaceship stopped in front of an enormous ring of copper and gold colour. The metallic circle was suspended there. At that moment, Lilith's aquamarine eyes had a reptile pupil. She had a long soft aquamarine dress fixed to her body. Lilith had on her blonde hair a platinum crown with embedded diamonds. On her left wrist she had a red leather thin bracelet. On her right wrist, Lilith had a gold bracelet, which had fixed topaz and emeralds. In addition, she had golden shoes, tied on her ankles by small and crossed straps.

She touched one topaz of her right bracelet. Then, the inner area of the giant ring circumference started filling by a spiral cloud of gold and turquoise colour. From that cloud left a platform of silver colour.

Lilith descended from her airship, and she started walking there. Suddenly, a spiral of black pieces appeared behind her. They rounded the queen and became stardust, which started to vanish. After that, Lilith appeared on a black superbike. She was wearing a black leather dress of a bike pilot.

Lilith turned on the engine and rolled on the platform towards the centre of the ring, which was a space-time portal. The girl accelerated her motorcycle very fast, and its tires creaked so loud pulling out smoke.

At the other side of that portal, Lilith arrived at the interior of an office in the Daedric Bank building at its topmost part. She was quickening her superbike towards the windows of that skyscraper. A sinusoidal wave explosion occurred when the superbike got through that window. A rain of broken glasses started falling from there. The black dressed pilot held her superbike and gave a tremendous and supernatural jump. Then, she fell onto the top part of another skyscraper. Lilith made it several times until arriving at the terrace of a parking building. There, she went towards the first floor of that edifice descending by the ramp for cars. Her task was to arrive at the Beliar High School zone.

The sun started getting an orange colour. A diplomatic caravan of three limousines with two Black Earth flags on its frontal part and six motorcycles was approaching there. Lilith was seeing the convoy and then, she left a mini rocket launcher from her superbike. Lilith triggered her weapon against one of the limousines and then, that car exploded. That was the caravan of Messrs Paulge, Thade, and Raw. The superbike pilot still had her black helmet on her head.

"Zen sheer naa wop yub loose am," Lilith said after that explosion.

She took her superbike and rolled on again. Many city patrols started pursuing and shooting at her. Lilith made circular and transparent gel shields with her left hand. She sent them through the air and the patrols crashed and exploded into those translucid barriers.

At the same time, Lilith was dodging the bullets coming from other patrols. The black leather dressed girl had arrived at one highway, which carried towards the high school area. Soon, she started seeing the castles and left the big highway and went towards the small and peaceful streets Beliar High School.

Once at the school campus, Lilith stopped her superbike in front of a red-haired girl. That teenager was the same who left the explosive device in a trashcan of Beta Persei Complex at the Molog Region (the day Lilith stole a Death Angel). The Queen of the Nymphs took off her black helmet and saw the grey eyes of that girl.

"It was so difficult for you to carry this undercover mission. It is not, my little girl?"

"Yes, my queen," the girl answered her and looked at her tenderly.

Lilith touched with her left hand the white right cheek of the red-haired girl.

"Today your mission is already completed."

She gave her a courtesy.

"My queen, here is the blood of the punisher."

The red-haired girl gave Lilith a refrigerated test tube, which contained a sample of Starlight's blood.

At that moment, Lilith launched a big gel shield with her right hand towards some arriving patrols. Those vehicles crashed into it creating a big explosion. A military chopper was approaching as well. Then, Lilith launched another shield upwards to avoid the shots from the helicopter.

"Now, come with me, my dear," Lilith said to the red-haired girl.

"Yes, my queen."

The sky had a gold-orange colour by the afternoon sun's reflection on the clouds. At that moment, the shade of the castles of Beliar High School contrasted against the green of the hills and the golden colour of the Gehenaesis River.

Near there, a white dove flew in front of a sniper that was pointing his weapon directly at Lilith. A bullet fired by that sniper travelled towards that place. Suddenly, the black fractal particles appeared again.

"*As upme*," Lilith said.

A small portal opened there. The Queen and the red-haired girl vanished. At the other side of the time-space vortex near the Nymph's planet, appeared those two girls.

They were in front of the big ring filled by the spiral clouds of turquoise colour. They were embraced when Lilith noticed that her hands were wet. She saw them; her hands were bathed in green blood.

"Please, forgive me, my queen," the red-haired girl said to Lilith, seeing her with sadness.

Then, she flopped on the silver platform, whilst her green blood flowed. Lilith gave a big scream and started crying quietly, and her tears ran down on her precious face. Soon, a spaceship arrived there. Many Nymphs descended from it and then they took the red-haired girl's body.

The Queen of the Nymphs wore an aquamarine dress.

"My queen. Now, what are we going to do?" one of the Nymphs said to Lilith.

"Our mission is to save the planets, not to all those inferior races that extinguish their own worlds. They just want to destroy life. We need killing them," Lilith said with rage and anger.

"But, my queen," another Nymph said to Lilith.

"I gave an order to kill the Hur-Appeans!"

"Yes, my queen," they answered.

All the Nymphs on that planet started executing Lilith's disposition, whilst their Queen went towards her fortress.

One of the Nymphs carried some of Starlight's blue blood. Another girl took from the turquoise colour box kept by the dragon-gargoyle a spot of silver dust. Those two Nymphs arrived at an energy reactor and poured both the dust and the blue blood into a special device there. The power source started functioning at its maximum capacity. The reactor was generating clean energy for the combat airships of Lilith's army.

Many silver combat spaceships started taking off from the runways of various military bases of Nymph's orb. Soon, those war airships reached the thermosphere of Lilith's planet and then, the portal ring.

A Nymph wore a white astronaut dress (it was for protocol because the Nymphs could breathe in the vacuum). The astronaut Nymph was attached to a silver spaceship. She started pouring other drops of the stolen blue blood on the giant metallic ring. Suddenly, the ring started circulating counterclockwise and the aquamarine inner portal became dark blue. At that moment, all the spaceships started passing through the blue hole. In that way, they arrived at the thermosphere of the Sattrin Earth immediately.

The Nymph's army airships were of three classes. First were called the Hawks, which were triangular with pliable delta wings and silver colour. They had at their top part heavy laser weapons.

The second airship class was the Daemons. They were bigger than the Hawks. They carried many Hawks, crews, fuels, and ammunition. The Daemons had the shape of a massive silver conical cylinder. At their rear part, they had a big reactor of light built with a ring of copper colour. It rotated generating enough energy to have a great flight combat autonomy.

The last one class was the Lighters, which were three hundred sixty-nine times bigger than the Hawks. The Lighters carried many Hawks, Daemons, high-level crews, and all the systemized controls of the former two kinds of spaceships. The Lighters had the shape of enormous ovals, as semi elongated spheres of silver colour.

All those airships appeared near the Sattrin Earth planet. They surfed on the grey surface of the undestroyed asteroid belt part.

Lilith was seated on her throne in the fortress at the other side of the vortex.

"Finished them, now," Lilith gave the order.

Then from six Lighters allocated in the asteroid belt left sixty Daemons. From them left six thousand Hawks ready to attack the Black and South Earth borders.

The Hawks slid over the asteroid belt surface and then turned their trajectory to enter the troposphere of Sattrin Earth. Once there, they started attacking both the senator's militaries and Starlight's forces triggered green lasers. The Nymphs did not attack the Agnesii warriors.

The beaches of the Eschem Region at Olympus Sea were a scenario of a carnage. In the sky were the Hawks fighting against the Dragonflies and Death Angels. On the soil, were the Black Earth army performing attacks against the South Earth creatures.

Some Hawks were flying and shooting at Starlight, whilst he continued falling. One Dragonfly was flying below him. The pilot of that airship pressed a button, opening the principal gate. Starlight fell into that aircraft. The commander of that Dragonfly turned her head.

"My Lord. Are you alright?"

"Miss Flussman, I always trust in your pilot abilities," Starlight said to her.

"Thank you, my Lord."

The laser shots were a real trap for any combat airship regardless of its band. Another Dragonfly was dodging the green lasers from a Hawk and some shots from the tanks as well. Near there, one aircraft of the rebels was flying parallel to the natural wall (on the South Earth coast). That airship was firing its blue laser, whilst five Hawks were pursuing it. That Dragonfly made an evasive manoeuvre near the wall towards the beach. Those Hawks could not avoid the natural rock formation and crashed into it.

Near that zone, more Hawks were in a triangle arrangement shooting at the soldiers on the beach. At the same time, a group of Dragonflies arrived there to defend that area. Other Hawks were flying down from the stratosphere towards the conflict sector. Some of Starlight's airships arrived there and started shooting at those space intruders.

Dragonflies and Hawks had a spherical, transparent-gel shield, which made it difficult for the laser (greens or blues) to damage them. However, those shields were not indestructible. Once they received many shots, those protections started losing their performance. Except for the Black Earth Air Force, the other two military bands had the same technology either shields or laser weapons.

There were many airships exploding in the heavens from the laser impacts creating illuminated circles. The visual effect of those explosions was like spirals because the airships gave turns to fall.

Soon, the Black Earth Imperium Navy was arriving at the Olympus Sea. There were littoral combat ships (LCS), attack submarines (AS), destroyers (DYS), and amphibious attack ships (AAS). Sixty AAS were guarded by sixteen LCS and one hundred submarines.

The LCS and AAS were far enough apart from the border because the amount of Agnesii in the battlefield was increasing. The LCS got up their canyons calculating the trajectory of torpedoes to impact the wall. The missiles were leaving from the LCS weapons, whilst the Hawks and Dragonflies flew over them.

Many torpedoes launched from the littoral ships went in a semi-parabolic path through the air. Those missiles impacted the natural wall breaking a great part of it into a thousand pieces. However, the effect of that navy attack was creating a big hole in the wall. It made more creatures of the South Earth passing towards Black Earth easier.

Once the craft of those military frigates noted the error to shoot at the wall, they stopped doing it.

The Hur-Appeans did not know how many creatures there were in that territory. The big vegetation, the constant formation of super clouds, and the shadow of the asteroid belt made it difficult to have a view from the satellites of Black Earth. Even more, BESA technology could not determine the heat map of the south subcontinent because most of Agnesii lived underground.

The South Earth warriors had prepared a great surprise for the battle. Again, the sound of the Sattrin Horn made the border tremble. Then, from the broken wall appeared many giants ready to die in the battle.

The wind brought a loud sound like a swarm of wasps approaching the border. Suddenly, heaven was decorated with thousands of young dragons. The Agnesii never had used them because those flying creatures took centuries to have an adult age and the giants had been asleep during the same time. Those reptiles started launching fire from their snouts at the Dragonflies, Hawks, armoured tanks, and Black Earth soldiers.

Agnesii combatants advanced in total disorder moving their axes killing everything in their path. Many brigades of the new regime were fighting face to face with those creatures. The giants were walking, crushing either soldiers or Agnesii with their big feet. Furthermore, those grand beings had vast and deformed mallets, which were smashing everyone. The only way to kill them was shooting at their third eye, which was in their forehead of their unpleasant and menacing faces.

Then, the snuchkurls entered the scene, killing every soldier of Black Earth in the battle.

Some days passed and the border of the Eschem Region and the South Earth had a big colourful stain from the gore. The red blood was from Agnesii and Hur-Appeans, whilst the green blood was from the Nymphs. There were many dead bodies of all bands, and pieces of Dragonflies and Hawks as well. In addition, there were many rats, flies, and vultures due to the great number of bodies in decomposition.

The three tyrants (Messrs Paulge, Thade, and Raw) announced on television the success of the operation. They manipulated the media and made the Hur-Appeans believe the Empire army had the war under control. That was because the war still stayed in the Eschem Region. The war had not passed towards other regions of Black Earth yet. The truth about it was the battle could be held by the action of Starlight's rebels and their technology.

The tyrants were on direct television to all Black Earth. Senator Thade took the word.

"In our great benevolence. Today, we will give a temporary amnesty to the big terrorist and assassin of Black Earth, Mr Starlight. That is, because he had fought against the intruders of South Earth, under the supervision of our glorious army. However, that pardon will finish when the battle has ended. After that, the assassin Starlight will be taken to prison. Thank you and the gods bless us."

Starlight and a part of his rebels were recharging fuel and ammunition in a cavern rock system, in the north of the Eschem Region. The rebel's leader was watching the transmission on a hologram portable screen.

"That is a political scenario. We are not fighting under their supervision! We are fighting for our people! It does not matter what they said. The point is my fellows. Today is the day that we are going to finish this war!" Starlight said with a powerful voice.

"Yes, my Lord," the soldiers at his service said.

Starlight continued, "We must be stronger than ever because today our will is over the dark forces of destruction. Today we are the light of freedom for all the universes. Today our acts will change the trend of history and our own existence as well. Today is the return of the light of stars. Today we are the kings of the universe! Go for the victory!"

"For the victory!" each soldier exclaimed.

Then, all of them took their Dragonflies and left their hiding military base. They joined with many other rebel partners at the war zone again. More Death Angels and armoured tanks were arriving there as well. Over them, heaven had an orange-red colour. The network of the laser shots still was in the confrontation zone. Airships of both sides were dropping like flies.

CHAPTER THIRTEEN
The Imperial War

On the ground, the Agnesii were cutting the heads off soldiers with their rustic axes and swords. The starving and tired Black Earth militaries were still fighting. They stole the frontal machine guns from the fallen Dragonflies to shoot at the South Earth creatures. In face-to-face combat, most of the time, the brutal force of the Agnesii won. It happened when the soldiers had not charged their thieved laser weapons.

The flies, the dust, the pestilence, the airships that were falling, the lasers, and their vibration on the ground made it so difficult to combat. Black Earth militaries recovered their energy with few foods and an injection of a strange green substance given by the army. That inoculation gave them better performance in battle. Conversely, Agnesii fed with dead bodies of their peers that were on the soil.

Meanwhile, the three tyrants were seated on their luxury chairs in the Amon Room. They were talking about the situation.

"We had an attack against us days ago by a strange sniper on a motorcycle. Fortunately, we had doubles and similar limousines for our security. This is the perfect alibi. We have them where we want. It is time to execute the Thirty-three Code," Mr Paulge said.

"Well, that returns the light of the stars," Mr Raw said.

"So be it," Mr Thade said.

Then, they gave their servants the instruction to execute the code, which activated all the Black Earth nuclear weapon systems. They wanted to bomb South Earth territory and the Eschem Region as well.

The snuchkurls cannot travel towards the inner of the Black Earth because its bones started failing, and their breathing system as well. It was due to the change of atmospheric pressure between the north and south environment of the Pandemonical Continent.

The big monsters that lived in the ocean and rivers of South Earth could not pass towards the north because the ocean soil was higher in Black Earth than South Earth. The bodies of those monsters and beings would rise over sea level, and they could not breathe.

Suddenly, most birds of Black Earth started having strange behaviour. Flocks of Ampelis and other birds were flying towards the north of Black Earth. Many animals of the same territory were snuggled in the soil. People were seeing this behaviour, but they did not know the reason for that situation.

Then, the three tyrants went towards the emperor's castle to have a secret assembly with the top military generals at their service. In the table at the principal dining room of that fortress, the militaries had allocated and installed a modern system of communications. Some hologram computers projected Sattrin Earth.

"My Lords, the protocol does not let any military activate the system for the Thirty-three Code. It must be activated by the emperor, but at this time I do not know…" one of those generals said.

"It is my duty as part of the new government to do that," Mr Thade interrupted him.

Then, he took from the general's left hand a golden key. It had a T-shape of three blades. Its shank was embossed with a helix line and its head was a kind of an ancient knocker.

Mr Thade pushed the key into a wireless silver box connected to the computers. Mr Thade turned the key. It made a small sound like a click.

"For the victory!" the tyrant said smiling.

"For the victory!" Messrs Paulge and Raw said as well.

All the militaries there started applauding in silence. Then, in each one of the thirteen BESA Headquarters started elevating big gates from the soil. There emerged white missiles with the flag of Black Earth and BESA insignias painted on them. The passages of each Hur-Appean territory decorated the background of the launching of those missiles. Each projectile left a stele of white colour behind them produced by their propellers. Those nuclear ogives had a semi-parabolic trajectory. All of them seemed like golden lines in heaven and were monitored from the castle by the militaries.

A great orchestra started playing a requiem, whilst people of thirteen regions were seeing the ogives furrowing the sky. Some prayed, others cried.

From her throne, Lilith was notified about the nuclear attack. She got very angry.

"That race does not understand anything about nature care. They just want to kill each other. Their sins must be purged! By the divine right imposed on me by all the universes and their creators; I order the Hur-Appean race must be removed from the face of Sattrin Earth."

The rest of the Nymphs started executing that order there. Immediately, all the Hawks left from Sattrin Earth. Then Daemons and Lighters started shooting to the entire orb from space. The white lasers of those two kinds of airships entered the blue planet. They started destroying the principal military bases and the cities of Black Earth and some ogives as well.

At that moment, Mr Aroth advised Starlight by his microphone,

"My Lord. The attack is coming from a part of the asteroid belt. The satellite showed me that there were many motherships, which were shooting at the planet. My Lord, intelligence found your parents in Befomet City Jail, and a team is leading the rescue…"

"Give me coordinates. I am going to go there personally," Starlight interrupted him.

"My Lord, is risking your travel there…"

"I said give me the coordinates."

"Yes, my Lord."

Then, Starlight's Dragonfly went so fast towards Befomet City. He was blinded by the feeling to save his parents and take them towards some safe place. He was dodging the white lasers that were entering from the sky. Behind him were four Dragonflies: Meletea, Aeda, Nemea, and General Stealth.

At that moment, in Sakopholus D'Moon City (capital of the Halocer Region and a city rounded by wild woods and jungles) entered a white laser coming from Nymph's army. It destroyed a part of a tall building with an angel shape in a stand-up position. A great part of that metropolis was destroyed as well.

In Mándala Heian Sun City in the Alucah Region, the white ray fell on the Supreme Volcano creating an eruption. A great column of magma and fire rocks furrowed the sky going towards Mándala Heian Sun City.

Armeninov-Gord City, capital of the Ahriman Region, received another heaven ray. It destroyed a great part of the city castles, whose roofs had shapes like coloured domes and globes.

Blue-Ice City, capital of Ahvitchi and the fjords region was touched with the light punishment, destroying the governor's castle.

Agoras Classical City capital of the Dumah Region saw as its constructions near the shore were falling like toy pieces by the white laser.

Pyramidal City, capital of the Eschem Region was the first to receive the divine touch of the Nymphs. Before the laser started destroying the pyramids, from their picks left a light towards the Ophiuchus Constellation. Then, those pyramids exploded into a thousand pieces.

In Hur-Appean Reich City capital of the Kheter Region, the killer ray destroyed many castles and the big monument, which had the inscription:

In gott wir vertrauen.

In Sanctus Imperium City, capital of the Viechtisha Region, the revenge of the Nymphs continued falling on the Templi Ominum Abba. The attack made the temple's golden dome tumble to the floor. That cupola gave many turns, breaking some constructions along its path.

Golden City, capital of the Rofacaler Region where the main banks of Black Earth were, felt the rigor of the fury of the space maidens as well. A white ray destroyed the railway track, which crossed that city parallel towards the Helvetica River.

In New-Light City the white laser destroyed the main square park, where was the big tower made of bronze with the inscription on its base:

La ville du lumière.

In Sanct-Real City, capital of the Habraxas Region, the Black Earth Temple was atomised, when the sky ray destroyed its white dome. Near there, in Beliar Stadium was playing an Eamun Disk match, when another ray fell on the rectangular field.

In Be Alpha Men City, capital of the Molog Region, the most important art galleries at Memorial Pace-Park Avenue were ruined by another white laser. In that city there was a statue of Be Alpha Men and its inscription in its base:

The wisdom will return the light of the empire to us.

That sculpture was broken in two parts by the wave of the explosion.

Starlight and his friends arrived at the coordinates given by Mr Aroth. It was a specific place of Befomet City jail. From their combat aircrafts, Starlight and General Stealth dropped a rope. Then, those braves descended by the cords, whilst all the Dragonflies continued unmovable there.

The prison was a fortress of grey colour and republican architecture. That construction was a library many centuries before. The clear grey colour of its walls contrasted against the brown colour of its roof. There was a big lake rounding the set of buildings of that jail.

The two rescuers fell on the roof of the fortress and started to run. They wanted to find the principal yard. The two friends arrived at the first floor of that building, whilst many inmates were running trying to escape. In that chaos, Starlight's adoptive father had escaped from his cell. He had arrived at the women's prison pavilion, where he could find his wife. The ex-congress chairperson saw his parents in the edifice in front of his location at the other side of the inner yard. They were hugging themselves. That couple saw his son as well. Starlight's mother sent him a kiss, whilst his father made the ancient greeting.

"Come on friend! We must go there!" the leader of the rebels said to General Stealth.

A few seconds later a great clatter sounded, and a white ray fell on the central yard. Starlight just could see a column of debris, then all was obscurity. A moment after, an orange light disturbed the closed eyes of Starlight. It was the last sunshine of the afternoon of that day crossing the dust.

Starlight was still stunned by the impact. He just could hear a great whistle. Then, the young man fainted.

The hours passed and steps of soldiers sounded on the fragments of concrete and iron at the destroyed jail. Some militaries of the senators' regime were dressed in anti-radiation clothes. They arrived at the location where Starlight and General Stealth were. The imperial militaries were putting dead bodies on a wheelbarrow to burn them. Starlight could not move and fainted again. He and Mr. Stealth were carried and offloaded by the senator's soldiers on a pile of dead people's bodies.

On the next day, the wet sensation together with a strong gasoline odour made Starlight wake up. He did not know how long he fainted. Starlight turned his head and saw General Stealth dead.

The stunned rebel tried getting up but without success. At that moment, a government soldier noticed that

Starlight was alive and ran towards him. That military looked at him and screamed at other new regime soldiers.

"Hey, there is one rat alive."

So, that official started hitting Starlight, and then other militaries arrived there to make the same thing. The sunshine started appearing in the sky. Starlight was suffering the beating when he turned his head. He saw his parents in another pile of dead bodies near where he was. Suddenly, his neck started moving as if Starlight had an insect under his skin.

Meanwhile, there was an assembly chaired by Versaria the Witch on Nymph's planet. That meeting was in Lilith's fortress. In that session was Mrs Versaria together with six ancient Nymphs seated in royal chairs behind a big table. The assembly room had a roof decorated with a hologram view of all constellations. The sunlight was entering there creating channels of multicolour dust. In that place, there were bleachers where the members of the justice council were seated. In the centre of the room was Lilith.

Mrs Versaria had on her right shoulder her big white owl. Then, the witch stood up and looked at Lilith fixedly.

"In this plasma universe Draconenans made the solar war to dominate the universe. The rest of the races of this universe won that war against them creating the universal peace agreement. I am the representative of the Arcans, the race that keeps the agreement between Draconenans, Manthises, Nymphs, Spectrans, and Clonades. I had cited this meeting because that agreement was broken. The

Nymphs' army had violated that treatment to intervene in Sattrin Earth with excessive use of force. You gave the order to kill millions of Loreans—the beings who dwell on that planet. In this case the self-named Hur-Appeans. You, Lilith the queen of the Nymphs had made an interstellar attack against an underdeveloped planet. I guess that you do not know the seriousness of this matter."

Lilith was still in silence looking at her judge.

Mrs Versaria continued, "The most powerful and dangerous race, the Draconenans, dominated this universe for aeons. That happened until the other races evolved and got enough technology to defend themselves. Sometime afterwards, the Manthises and the Spectrans become Draconenans allies. A diplomatic Manthis, the big grey insectoid race fell in love with a Spectran princess. A big-winged reptile Draconenans general, helped the couple to prolong those feelings for eternity using Arcan's technology. They mixed their DNA and created the fruit of their love, a Ketherus. In fact, that is the mix called Essence of the Universe, which is guarded by the Nymphs in Pandora's Box. The cubic container was allocated on this planet and kept by the dragon-demon. The son of that new DNA had the capability to destroy all universes and at the same time to kill the body, which we live in. Now, a new Ketherus is between us. Arcans and Nymphs created a race called Asdomii to control the Ketherus. We choose the best Asdomii and that being is you, Lilith. However, you cannot kill or hurt the Ketherus. Your duty was to control him and not release his powers."

"Him?" Lilith asked.

"That new replica is the emperor of the Ketherus. He had lived here during this aeon."

"He is the most powerful evil being in the universe. Over more, the Ketherus created the Leviathans. That race govern the Loreans created by the nasty Draconenans. Those Loreans or Hur-Appeans, tortured my descendants converting them into Agnesii," replied Lilith.

"His DNA saved your life many times," Versaria interrupted her.

"What?"

"The day that you arrived at Sattrin Earth in one of your multiple rebirth forms. Your spaceship lost control colliding with the caravan of the Ahvitchi governor. A few years before the same happened with Starlight. His adoptive parents took him to the doctor. There, fortunately, we obtained his blood, and we used it to help you in the accident. Almost, we lost you at that time. Starlight's blood came back to you from the dead. Moreover, his body fluid had helped to develop all Nymphs' technology for a long time."

"That means nothing," replied Lilith again.

"That means you broke a universal peace agreement. You broke the oath to not kill the races of a planet. You broke the most important rule of the Arcans, Nymphs, and Asdomii. That rule is to be merciful. The Nymphs' justice council had deliberated. We decided to put you in jail immediately."

At that moment, the white owl flew towards Lilith. It converted into a black owl opening its big claws and trapped Lilith. The bird started fusing with her. That new ameboid and deformed being gave a guttural scream saying, "*Asas upme.*"

Suddenly, a blue light emanated from that being. Then, it broke into a thousand pieces. Those fragments on the floor joined and formed the white owl, which was dead.

All the people in the room jumped from their chairs to take Lilith. Behind her, many black fractal pieces appeared there. She disappeared from that room saying, "This is my body. You fool."

"She wanted to kill the body in which we live!" Versaria exclaimed.

Then, Lilith appeared in front of the circular vortex outside her planet. She took one of her diamonds and cut herself scattering her green blood over the vortex. The portal was activated and then Lilith passed through it. At the other side, she was ready to continue guiding her troops for the attack against Sattrin Earth.

Meanwhile, from Starlight's blue eyes dropped many tears seeing his father and mother dead. The young man turned his head to see the lifeless body of General Stealth. He still had his eyes opened. Starlight could not close them because he was getting hit by the soldiers. The movements of Starlight's neck were faster than before. His eyes changed to black colour, both his iris and sclera. In his brain, chains of green DNA were produced. The movements under his neck skin started creating in all his body. His voice became guttural, and his muscles started growing slowly. The sunlight each time illuminated his new grey skin.

The soldiers started running, scared by Starlight's transformation. His back broke at the topmost part and started leaving an exoskeleton, which was covered by his blood. Suddenly, Starlight had become a giant gargoyle.

He had dragon wings of dark-grey colour, muscle body, and horns. Starlight looked like his costume in South Earth, but bigger. At that moment, he remembered his jet accident so well. His plane exploded giving many turns. His Agnesii costume left the plane burning it together with its suitcase. Starlight had not camouflaged during his travel through Agnesii lands. He had converted into the same being that was appearing now. His wings helped him to escape from the South Earth horde the day of the flood.

The shiny body of the dark winged demigod was in a stand-up position. Starlight made a signal putting his right hand index and middle finger pointing towards the ground. A spherical wave left the soil rounding him and his dragon wings started moving. It seemed as if Sattrin Earth was stopping, whilst the dust particles and some drops of water were ascending as Starlight did. The gargoyle-demon was elevating over the ruins of the penitentiary with the sunshine falling on his wings and back. Regardless, he had legs with claws that were menacing-looking—strong and beautiful at the same time.

Starlight flew until he reached the thermosphere and saw the fleet of Nymphs' combat airships. That monster opened his snout and launched to those spaceships a golden ray as a big laser. All at once, some Lighters were shooting at him. All those impacts were on Starlight producing an enormous bright. Then, that monster took all that energy and started condensing it into a small ball, which held in his right-hand-palm. After it, he ate that energy sphere.

Meanwhile, in Nymphs' fortress, Mrs Versaria gave the order to find Lilith in any place of the universe.

One of the servants Nymphs asked, "My lady. What is the meaning of the body in which we live?"

At that moment, Mrs Versaria approached her.

"My dear, the fractal theory says that everything is a scale model of everything. The same is a solar system as an atom. *Quod est superius est sicut quod inferius, et quod inferius est sicut quod est superius.* In our veins and blood, there are as many molecules as infinite galaxies. They live in us as we live in one kind of live form. We are its proteins and viruses at the same time. As above, so below."

"Are we like microbes?" the servant asked.

"Yes, but we are the body for others. Each superior body is known as a plasma universe," Mrs Versaria answered.

That servant took the voice again, "My lady. We the Nymphs control the space, which means that we rule the body. It is not?"

"Yes, my dear. Meanwhile, the Spectrans govern the time," Mrs Versaria said.

"Thank you, my lady," the servant said to Mrs Versaria.

The witch continued her path and met with other members of the justice council. One of those Nymphs had a beautiful black face, blue eyes, and blonde hair. "My Lady, we are going to hold a meeting again. The escape of the queen activated the change crown protocol," she said to the witch.

"*D'accord.*"

The Nymphs' took their seats, and the council started the session again. One ancient Nymph of red hair got up and pronounced with a strong voice, "Due to the last events, the total of the members of the council have accorded that Versaria the Arcan witch is going to be crowned as queen of the Nymphs temporarily."

The great witch was in front of the council. "The will of the council is my will. Your knowledge will bless me, and your thoughts and prayers will guide me," Queen Versaria said.

"Long live the queen," all members in the council said.

At that moment, another Nymph was arriving there. Then, she gave a courtesy to Versaria.

"My queen. The being called Starlight has taken his real form."

"We must activate all our defence systems. We must avoid that he or his real soldiers arrived at this part of the universe. Where is he?" the new queen asked.

"In front of our troops on Sattrin Earth."

"Withdraw our troops from that location, now!"

All servants started running to execute the order of the recent queen. Then, the Nymphs of the council and Queen Versaria left the fortress.

There were three silver spaceships in front of that construction. The council was divided into three groups and each one took one of those airships.

In her transportation, the queen started talking with one of the members of the council of her group, "I hope that Starlight had not sent a warning sign to the Draconenans, Manthises or Spectrans."

"They could take this situation as an opportunity to take control of the universe again," the Nymph replied.

"Yes, I hope that Starlight has not settled his troops yet."

"My queen, I do not understand. The Hur-Appeans; I meant the Loreans at Starlight's service have not the technology to arrive here. In that case, they cannot fight against us nor breathe in space."

"I am not referring to the Loreans. I refer to the Leviathans, his DNA troops. Squadrons created by cryobiology. During aeons on each universe cycle, the replicas of the supreme Ketherus generate their own militia. Each one of those cycles changes their space-time properties to produce a new life era. The inferior beings as the Loreans know it like a Big Bang. Basically, it is a reorder of the light. That event creates beings such as Starlight or Lilith and a big network of fractal multiverses."

"So the Ketherus, like him, create the Leviathans."

"That is correct."

"My queen. I do not understand. If Starlight created the Leviathans, who found the Black Earth territories before Starlight appeared here? So, do you think that there is more than one Starlight?"

"I hope not, my dear. He was created by unnatural means, as I said before. However, on each universe cycle he is cloned many times by his allies. They do it in that way to have control of the universe."

"My queen. Do you refer to his allies as Manthises, Draconenans, and Spectrans?"

"That is right."

At that moment, Starlight was launching the golden ray from his snout again shooting at Nymphs' spaceships. They were exploding one by one, by that ray. Meanwhile, some of those combat airships started to return from that place.

The Nymph that was talking with Queen Versaria received a calling. She made a bow to her queen and then took her hologram phone, "Hello... Well, I am going to inform her now. Thank you."

The Nymph looked at Versaria.

"My queen, Starlight destroyed more than half of our troops in the Sattrin Earth's asteroid belt. In addition, intelligence notifies us that the pyramids of Black Earth sent a signal towards the Ophiuchus Constellation before being devastated."

The witch just held her chair so hard.

"This cannot be the end of everything. Please, you call intelligence to find the possible replicas of Starlight in this universe."

Meanwhile in Befomet City, Mr Aroth was in the rebels' headquarters. He was trying to get information about Starlight, General Stealth, and the girls. From one of the hologram screens, he received a calling.

One rebel said to him, "Commander Aroth, here sixteenth troop leader. We rescued three survivors of three falling airships. The pilots, Aeda, Nemea, and Meletea are alive but wounded. The airships of General Stealth and our lord were destroyed by the attack of the Nymphs. The general is dead, I confirm, he is dead. We found the body of General Stealth and the parents of our lord. However, we have not found our master yet. Everything is debris here. We need aerial support. What is the next order, Commander?"

Mr Aroth was so confused and stunned by that notice. However, he took a second breath to resolve that situation. He said to that rebel on the battlefield, "I am going to send you seven Dragonflies for support. Please, send me the coordinates. I need those girls in safe conditions now!"

"Sir, yes sir," the rebel answered him.

Mr Aroth was starting to cry when he noticed an increasing energy on his screens. He watched them and started smiling.

"My Lord is alive," he said to himself.

At the same time, in one room of the governor's castle were just the three senators. They were watching on the hologram screens, the image of the Starlight in the Sattrin Earth's troposphere. The television channels still were broadcasting all the events of that war.

Senator Thade took the word, "Fellows, our mission is complete. In this way, we kept the boy until he released his natural powers. He is the first of our lineage, who has reached that level. All of us helped him to be safe in this universe. We helped him to grow as well. We must be happy because this war would give us our promised reward. Our Lord will be so happy for all this."

At that moment, a being like a death shadow entered there.

"In fact, I am," the masculine voice said.

The death shadow put off his worn out black robe. Under that tunic appeared a silhouette of a man, who wore a helmet and a cape. His helmet was made of gold, and it had slots of turquoise colour for his eyes and nose. Some of his blond hair appeared from the bottom part of its metal hood. He put it off denoting that hair was glued to the helmet. That old man was the emperor. In fact, that was the first time that he showed his appearance. He had plenty of hoary hair and a white face. His eyes had a blue-sky colour.

He had the figure of an elderly Starlight. The three senators made a curtsy to him.

"My Lord."

That old Starlight was one of the Ketherus replicas that had arrived in that universe before.

He looked at the senators. "Fellows, during all this time we had worked together to obtain the change of the universe. Today, we got it. For that purpose, we arrived here from the Ophiuchus Constellation. So, I am to reward you as promised. We are going to return towards our home. Soon, the young Starlight will wake up our warrior brothers. Our soldiers who came from our blood. My fellows, you helped him in all his process to be the leader of this planet. The young Starlight was blinded by his fear and anger. That irrational behaviour made the course of the universe be in our favour," the old Starlight said.

"Yes, my Lord. The wisdom of our universe is magnificent," Mr Paulge said.

Meanwhile, on the ruins of the asteroid belt of Sattrin Earth, Starlight continued destroying Lilith's army. At that point, a big portal opened there. The Nymphs' airships still in combat started withdrawing. One of them was shooting at Starlight to prevent him from advancing through the portal. However, he wrecked all airships before they could traverse the vortex. Then, the portal closed so fast.

Starlight was alone in that part of the universe. Rounding him were just the fragments of the enemy airships and the asteroid belt. Those wreckages were falling towards Sattrin Earth by effect of its gravity.

From the border of Black Earth and South Earth, it was possible to see those stellar rubbles entering the planet. It was like a rain of fire. On the ground, the Nymphs' rays had destroyed more than half of Black Earth. Many dead animals and birds were everywhere. Moreover, thirteen missiles of N-load of 66MT were launched on Agnesii location, from Black Earth. Then, the mantle of destruction and the grey radioactive clouds covered an enormous part of the Pandemonical Continent. Thousands of Agnesii were dead on their territory.

Starlight continued seeing the magnificence of the universe when a little point of light started appearing near him. That shine grew, revealing a spiral way and then a big dark turquoise disk of light. Lilith left in a stand-up position from there.

Her size was bigger, like Starlight. She had a shiny golden armour fitted to her body. Suddenly, her back started bleeding. Golden wings grew from her. She had a big bracelet on her left wrist. Lilith had golden metal gloves as well. Once her golden wings had grown completely, she looked at Starlight with her aquamarine eyes. "You Ketherus spawn, son of the betrayal and the nasty Draconenans, Manthises, and Spectrans. Today, is the day you die!"

From her right glove left a double light as a rod made of a laser. She activated her left bracelet, which became a Tyet weapon.

Starlight saw her. "Do you believe that all my hatred could be contained? No, I just want to see your Asdomii rotten body scattered throughout the universe. You killed my family, so I am going to destroy you!"

Then, he pointed his right index and middle finger towards his feet and a transparent energy sphere appeared around him. At the same time, thousands of strange beings from various crypts started waking up in a secret cryobiology laboratory belonging to Beliar High School. They were the same crystal coffins that Lilith used to visit. Some of those beings had eagle peaks, other owls, lions, goats, and wolves' heads. Those creatures started leaving from the translucid vaults flying towards the sky. They were riding alicorneus (winged horses with horns), and shedus (winged lions with a cheetah head). Those winged beings were hidden in crypts in that laboratory as well. Once, those monsters were flying in the in Befomet City heaven people were scared again. They did not know if those beings would start another battle.

Soon, Starlight was rounded by those creatures. They were his own army, the Leviathans. Meanwhile, Lilith made a sign as a circumference with her left hand and thousands of turquoise energy circles appeared around her. From them left many winged Nymphs loyal to Lilith. They had the same laser and Tyet weapons as their leader. Those Nymphs were against Queen Versaria as well.

"This is my space. You spawn," Lilith said to him with a robotic voice.

"This is my time, you Asdomii," Starlight said.

The two armies were in front of each other; the imperial war had started. Starlight made a sign with his right hand. He pointed his index and middle right-finger upwards. Due to that action, in the BESA Headquarters at Befomet City the soil started to tremble. Suddenly, from that place left a blade (Starlight's fencing sword). It seemed like a silver missile going to the sky. Then, Starlight put his left hand over his forehead. There he was, creating little thunders, which produced a small gemstone of cyan colour. He took it with his hand and observed it so focused. At that moment, the sword arrived there. Starlight embedded the gem at the sword and the latter started growing to form an enormous warrior blade. Then, Starlight and Lilith jumped over their troops and started to fight between them. Each time that Lilith's laser weapon hit Starlight's sword the impact created a massive transparent sinusoidal wave. A kind of orchestrated music sounded in the outer space where the battle was occurring. Starlight and Lilith seemed like they were dancing in space with each defence and attack movement.

Meanwhile on Sattrin Earth, the absence of the asteroid belt made the sea tides decontrolled. The women and the females of each breed of birds and animals started feeling dizzy. It was caused by the change in the tide and the planet's electromagnetic field. Sattrin Earth started suffering strong earthquakes. In all that chaos, the emperor continued with his three loyal senators in the castle.

"My Lord, it is time," Mr Thade said.

"Yes, my friends. Now, I am going to give each one of you the promised reward."

Then, the emperor raised his right hand and touched so fast in a sequence his index, middle and ring fingers with his thumb finger. Immediately, from the emperor' waist left various tentacles. Those appendices entered by senators' mouths, ears, and noses. The three politicians whitened their eyes while, black tears as oil stained their faces. From their foreheads left a ameboid light form, which was trapped by other emperor's tentacles.. Then, the senators lay dead on the floor.

"Now, I must find the girls and Mr Aroth. The only one lord of this universe is me. I must annihilate all Starlight's replicas, their allies, and servants as well. I am the Farmer, the only supreme Ketherus. The universe must be on its knees in front of me!" the emperor said to himself.

In a distant planet called Belathrix in the Ophiuchus Constellation were leaving from that place thousands of white spaceships with the shape of an oval. It was because that army received the signal from the pyramids of the Eschem Region. At the other side of the universe, near Sattrin Earth a circular vortex opened again. Just a silver airship was travelling through the portal. On it was the new queen of the Nymphs and her delegates. That spaceship had painted an insignia of Arcans race. It was a red circle decorated with a feminine form with wings, two lions, one snake, and two owls at its sides. Queen Versaria knew that Lilith was near Sattrin Earth and wanted to go there to put her under arrest.

Starlight moved so fast as if he was teleporting himself. Then, he appeared near the portal trespassing it.

At the same time, the spaceship of Nymphs' queen left that vortex to arrive at the outer space of Sattrin Earth. Starlight approached that instant, and he crossed it. A moment later, the portal closed.

At the other side of the copper coloured space-time portal, the Ketherus had arrived near Nymphs' planet. Immediately in that orb sounded an alarm in every city. Many civil and military spaceships started leaving from that planet. There were Lighters, Hawks, and Daemons leaving as well.

"I see will you fall wherever you may roam," Starlight said.

At that moment, he opened his snout and launched his golden ray against that green planet. His mortal light hit the orb's troposphere creating a blue Aurora Borealis. Then, the ray crashed into the soil, raising an immense column of rocks into flames. That pillar of debris was increasing its diameter, whilst near there were many Nymphs praying and singing in chorus, *"Zen sheer naa wop yub loose am."*

The wave of the impact was destroying everything on that planet-green jungles and cities. Dynamic skyscrapers, dome constructions, and flying autos were pulverized by the expanding mortal ripple. The column of destruction arrived at the fortress where Pandora's Box and the dragon-demon were. Then, a great sound trembled with strength in that place and the magma started entering there by its basal part. The dragon got burned by the magma. The box exploded and a silver fluid left that cube-shape container as a volcanic eruption. All that silver and viscous liquid left the planet and entered Starlight's nose.

He looked at one of three waning crescent moons of that planet. The silver fluid made a supernova explosion in Starlight's brain and his DNA as well. He started screaming, his skin changed to a golden colour. His eyes transformed from black to aquamarine in a slow way. Then, he went towards the sun of that planetary system as teleporting there. Starlight hugged that sun and then ate it. At that point, he was the most powerful being in the universe.

Starlight closed his eyes and took a breath like releasing from a burden. Then, he made a sign with his right hand as a circle creating a vortex of golden colour and then passed through it.

Starlight appeared at the battle zone again. Lilith saw him from above and went to kill him. Starlight looked upwards to see her. Both armies were fighting, forming concentric cycles and at their centre was Lilith as a vanishing point. There were many stars and a waning crescent moon behind her, it seemed like she was standing on the moon. She was raising her right arm holding her destroyer laser. Starlight teleported and then was in front of Lilith. He took his sword and cut Lilith's laser weapon, breaking it into two parts. She saw her laser weapon broken and felt very scared. Starlight was ready to kill her.

At that moment, she modified her Tyet weapon's shape from a bracelet to a knot shape. Lilith stabbed Starlight with her metallic artefact in the right side of that golden gargoyle. The weapon started suctioning his blue blood. He looked at her with his new aquamarine eyes and smiled. At that point, his blood was returning to his body through that weapon. In fact, Lilith's green blood was suctioned by Starlight by means of that Tyet. He was mentally controlling Lilith's weapon.

All Nymphs were using their Tyets against Starlight's army members as well. However, the inverse suction effect occurred for all Tyets, Starlight was to control them. Therefore, Lilith's army was diminishing in a faster way.

Suddenly, thousands of golden circles appeared near the battle. From them left many oval white airships of the Stellar Alliance (Draconenans, Manthises, and Spectrans). Those spaceships had a Nebra's insignia painted on them. It was a dark turquoise rectangle decorated with many golden stars and a sun.

Queen Versaria noted that event from her airship, which was near there. "Thank gods. Now we can stop this chaos," she said to herself.

Then, she ordered her airship crew to go towards the mothership of the alliance. Once there, Queen Versaria and her delegates (five Nymphs), went to meet with the leading members of the alliance. There were many Clonades working in that enormous oval ship because they were created by the Manthises to be at their service. The Clonades were beings of mid and tall height, of silver colour, almost transparent with big black eyes. They were dressed in armours of violet colour. They made the receiving protocol for Versaria and her group. The

Nymphs' queen and her entourage were escorted towards the principal room. The interior of that office was white with doors in aluminium and glass. There were hologram screens showing many places of different universes.

Soon, Queen Versaria was in front of the Universal Council. Morhax (the representative of Draconenans) was dressed in a silver scarf and a skirt of the same colour. He had a clear grey and scaly skin. He had a strong and naked figure with toned muscles. His face was like a Lorean with scales. He had a reptile tongue and no feet. Instead, he had a long and thick tail. He had a gold mask on his forehead and eyes. It was embossed with two serpents entwined around a rod. Morhax had horns, hands with long claws, and four big bat wings on his back. The representative of the Manthises called Beriht and had an insectoid appearance. Her eyes were yellow and she wore a green cape and an exoskeleton of white colour. Her skin was dark grey; she had four arms and four legs. The last one member of the alliance representatives was a Spectran, his name was Gremory. He was like a hologram projection. His skin was a mixture between a transparent and a soft green tone. He had a masculine appearance and had a guttural voice as well. Gremory had claws instead of hands, white dreads, and orange eyes. He wore a large white coat, which looked like a white death shadow.

"My apologies for all these disagreements," Queen Versaria said.

"We appreciated your bravery to come here, but one of your flunkies started a plasma war. For your information, Starlight destroyed the Nymphs' planet called Eurynomus," Mohrax said to her.

"Yes, I already had felt it when I arrived here."

The five blonde-haired and blue-eyed Nymphs did not know it. They left some tears wetting their diamond collars and semitransparent dresses.

Queen Versaria continued, "The same had happened during each universe cycle. It depends on each one of you if we start the fire."

Beriht took the word, "This plasma universe has no defence against us. We can change the course of time to our will. We created our own slaves giving them a certain degree of intelligence and soul, which is our feed. They give us conductive metals as gold and minerals like quartz. We had made it in many galaxies during aeons. We spend much of our time creating them and their worlds. However, as in the past one your Asdomii interfered with our farms. One of them, a young girl called Be Alpha Men, took half the population of our Loreans changing their DNA. She converted them into useless beasts called Agnesii. Now, another Asdomii destroyed our planet called Sattrin Earth. The Nymphs and the Arcans created that race just to violate our peace agreement. However, we put one of Ketherus' replicas as a leader of this universe. Therefore, you tell me. What is the reason to not eat you now?"

"Any, for all those I am here," Queen Versaria answered.

"Unfortunately, your high status does not let us devour you. We, the Stellar Alliance, respect the peace agreement. However, if we decided to destroy this universe once and for all, we can do it now. We agreed to leave you alive ancient Arcan, together with your delegates. The only one condition is that you take as a prisoner that Asdomii called Lilith and carry her so far from this side of our universe. The next time, we will have no consideration and will destroy everything," Gremory said to her.

"I accept the condition, but the same thing I say to yours."

Then, Queen Versaria and her entourage were escorted by some Clonades towards their spaceship. The Queen and her Nymphs left that mothership in their transportation.

Meanwhile, Starlight took his golden sword and made a second movement to cut Lilith into two parts. At that moment, his sword hit Lilith's transparent protection shield making a big sinusoidal wave. She had not activated it until Starlight broke her weapon because she was so confident about herself. The wave expansion finished destroying the asteroid belt and the artificial satellites of Black Earth. That impact killed the rest of the Nymphs loyal to Lilith. Opportunely, Starlight extended his left hand creating a protection field for his army avoiding the shock wave. The propagation of the impact started damaging the shield against the ultraviolet rays that rounded Sattrin Earth. The wave launched Lilith towards the Pandemonical Continent.

From Black Earth, the few alive people could see the fire rain produced by the debris of the asteroid belt arriving at the planet. There were many thunders in that grey sky because the ultraviolet rays and the dust were altering the atmosphere. At that moment, two big golden angels entered Sattrin Earth. The first was Lilith and the second was Starlight. He increased the speed of his flying to smash her against the soil of the Netflimt Region. Once they crashed into the ground, they created an explosion. That event created another wave expansion forming an enormous column of debris. The Pandemonical Continent was suffering floods, earthquakes, and volcanic eruptions. The radioactive wind was spreading over all the northern and southern territories. Many continental plates began moving with great strength destabilizing the rotary axis of that orb as well.

Meanwhile, the emperor was travelling in one military helicopter from his castle towards Royal Imperium University. Once he arrived there, he wanted to reach the deepest desk of the basement. In that level were Mr Aroth and the girls. The rebels loyal to young Starlight made a reverence to see the emperor. It was due to his face being the same as Starlight's, but much older. The emperor took advantage of it and made the sign with his hand to kill those rebels in the same way as the senators. At the same time, little fissures produced by the earthquakes on the walls of that fortress started forming. The magma from the centre of Sattrin Earth was trying to enter there because of the rupture of that planet's crust.

Starlight after pushed Lilith from the heaven to the soil, he flew towards the basement of the university. Lilith was she is badly injured and buried in a large crater in the ground created by the impact.

Once Starlight in his golden gargoyle form had arrived the university, he saw the emperor trying to kill his friends. Mr Aroth was in front of the three girls with his arms wide open to protect them. At that moment, the emperor turned his head. Then, he got on his knees.

"My Lord," he said to the golden Starlight.

"This appearance has made me understand and remember every event related to the creation of this plasma universe, the war, and the races. You stole my life. You let the Nymphs kill my master Malmo. You let me suffer in South Earth. You lie to the Hur-Appeans as emperor. Now, I choose to be the owner of my life. Today, I choose my destiny," Starlight said to the emperor.

"My Lord, I was just training you to unleash your powers and let you be the emperor of this plasma universe."

"I choose to do it by myself now," the golden gargoyle said.

"Fool, you will never greater than me…"

Therefore, the golden Starlight raised his left hand and touched so fast in a sequence his index, middle and ring fingers with his thumb finger. Immediately, from the golden gargoyle left various tentacles from his waist. Those appendices entered by the mouth, ears and, nose of his older doppelganger. The emperor whitened his eyes while, black tears as oil stained his face. From his foreheads left a triangle light form, which was trapped by other Starlight's tentacles.

Then, the emperor lay dead on the floor.

Starlight's friends were still staying quiet by the fear of seeing that big winged and golden gargoyle.

Just Mr Aroth dared asking, "My Lord?"

Starlight started changing his appearance to a normal Hur-Appean in a slow way. His eyes changed from aquamarine to blue colour and his sword changed its size and shape as well. A naked Starlight appeared in front of his friends.

"Where are Captain Thunder and Miss Flussman?" Starlight asked.

"They could not get it, my Lord," the girls answered.

Immediately, Mr Aroth ran to bring him a big black mantle, which was in one of the closets of that room. He covered Starlight with that blanket.

"Thank you, my friend. Each one of you has helped me in the hardest moments of my life. Now, it is my turn."

"Thank you, my Lord," all of them said to him.

"Meletea Vanety, you are very special to me. You advertised to me about the war, the emperor and all of this. Therefore, you are the chosen one."

Then, Starlight approached her, and he gave her a big hug and a kiss of love.

"This is my dream come true, my love," Meletea said to him.

At that moment, the rest of his friends were amazed seeing the passionate kiss. However, the magma started entering there by the wall fissures.

Starlight made a movement with his left hand as a circle. "I am going to take all my people towards my home. Now, I am the emperor of the universe. Now, I make the rules," he said to his friends.

There, a golden circle of energy appeared, and that group of partners vanished, whilst the basement started to burn. The same happened with all alive people of Black Earth. In front of each one of them appeared energy portals and soon those persons vanished as well. Then, the survivor Hur-Appeans, Starlight, and his friends appeared on the biggest spaceship of the alliance. There, the representatives of the three powerful races to see Starlight got on their knees. "My Lord," they said.

"My planet was destroyed. The radioactive footprint will not let us develop the life for these Hur-Appeans on that place again. At least, not for a long time. Therefore, as Emperor of this universe I decree that all alive Hur-Appeans go towards the planet called Belathrix."

"So be it, my Lord," Mohrax, Beriht, and Gremory said.

The people were so scared, and the children were crying.

Starlight turned to them. "My people, you do not have to be afraid, we are going to go home."

Then, he made a sign with his right hand and all Hur-Appeans fell asleep and started levitating. Starlight sent them towards the relaxation area of the spaceship.

Mohrax, Beriht, and Gremory gave the order to Clonades to get trip capsules for those Loreans. Then, the new Emperor transformed himself into the golden gargoyle again.

"I am going to help my warriors," he said to Mr Aroth and the girls with his new guttural and strong voice.

Starlight gave another kiss to Meletea and made a golden circle with his right hand to teleport himself towards outer space. A few seconds later, he appeared there in front of his army. "My Leviathans, see, hear and be silent because our heart is happy. We march to our home. We won," he said to them.

"*Meriah.*" they replied.

In ancient Ketherian that meant: we won.

Starlight made another golden circle and said, "*Zen sheer naa wop yub loose am.*"

At that moment, all of them disappeared together with their alicorneus, shedus, and the alliance spaceships as well.

Then, in the distance a light turned on there. It was Queen Versaria's spaceship, which was going towards Sattrin Earth.

Near the devastated and empty Befomet City was the hole made by the impact of Starlight and Lilith. The ex-leader of the Nymphs was alone, weak, and bleeding. Her Tyet weapon was broken. Suddenly, she changed the colour of her eyes from aquamarine to green and her wings started decreasing. The dusty soil around her seemed like a white velvet carpet. She was scared and sad.

"I lost everything," Lilith said to herself.

Her tears were wetting her face. She continued, "I was blinded by the anger. He did not kill my sister. I did it! My precious and little red-haired girl. I killed you. I am so sorry my dear. I think… I lost him. I know he loves me no more. Starlight my love. Why did you betray me?"

I never had betrayed you. she thought in her mind that Starlight's voice answered.

"Do you love me?" she asked herself again.

"Always," the imaginary voice answered.

Finally, Versaria's spaceship arrived there. Lilith covered her left eye due to the light of the airship. Then Queen Versaria left from her airship levitating. The image of the moon was behind her.

"I am sorry my queen, I was blinded," Lilith said to Versaria.

"At last, you understood it."

"Yes, my queen. I lost everything."

"I do not think so. The body in which we live is still vibrating. You are alive, and at least five Nymphs and me as well. We must rebuild all. So, you get up little girl."

"Thank you, my queen. Forgive me for all that I have done."

Lilith stood up with difficulty.

Versaria pronounced the following words, "*As upme.*" Then, they and their spaceship vanished from there.

The acid storm started to decompose everything: cities, woods, and jungles of the Pandemonical Continent. The Agnesii race was extinguished from that planet by the radioactive dust.

Few years later, all life forms in heaven and soil died. The ultraviolet rays finished destroying everything there. Sattrin Earth became a celestial colossus of red colour.

EPIGRAPH

Sometime afterwards, many alliance spaceships were entering and leaving from a blue planet. A military general had a white uniform with Nebra's insignia embroidered on her right arm. That blonde girl was on an oval spaceship. "Captain, the airships that trapped the Star LHD completed their mission to finish the artificial satellite. It is arriving at your location now," she said watching a hologram screen.

"My general. Roger that," a handsome black military man, who was in another spaceship answered her.

He had a microphone glued to his neck. Then that man changed the transmission channel.

"Fellows, our Emperor gave this mission to us: the Loreans' descendants," he said to some pilots, which were in other smaller spaceships.

"Roger that, captain," they said to him.

The captain changed the channel to talk with the general again, "General, I am seeing the satellite. It is big and rounded. Why does it have a big crater and many smaller ones as well?"

"The smaller are gates for our spaceships, and the big one is for the universal trigger. Our Emperor wants to avoid the events that occurred in Ares. This satellite will create the magnetic field of this farm as well."

"Yes, for the reproductive life cycle. General, before arriving at this location I noted a red planet near here. It is Ares, the ancient Sattrin Earth?"

"Yes, captain. Our Emperor named it by the great wars that happened there. By the way, have you got the Draconenan bacteria analysis?"

"Yes General. It takes less than a half aeon to develop the new race on this farm. The bacteria and the satellite will help us to do it."

"He has favoured our commencement. Okay captain, thank you. Roger that."

Be the light.

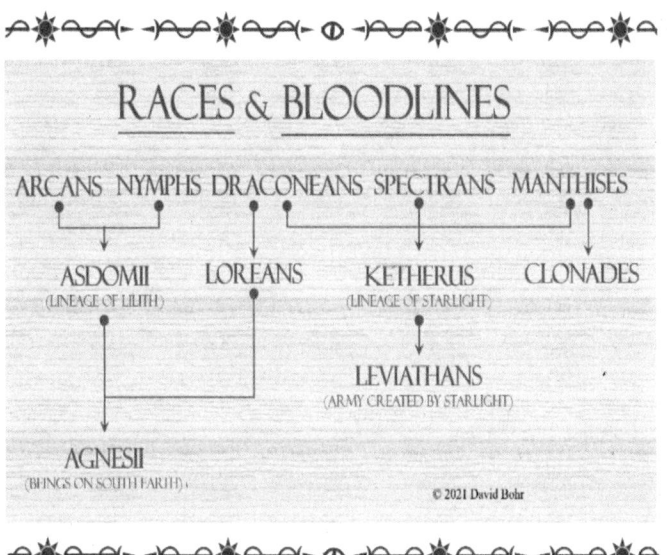